아직 일어나지 않은 일

아시아에서는 《바이링궐 에디션 한국 대표 소설》을 기획하여 한국의 우수한 문학을 주제별로 엄선해 국내외 독자들에게 소개합니다. 이 기획은 국내외 우수한 번역가들이 참여하여 원작의 품격을 최대한 살렸습니다. 문학을 통해 아시아의 정체성과 가치를 살피는 데 주력해 온 아시아는 한국인의 삶을 넓고 깊게 이해하는 데 이 기획이 기여하기를 기대합니다.

Asia Publishers presents some of the very best modern Korean literature to readers worldwide through its new Korean literature series 〈Bilingual Edition Modern Korean Literature〉. We are proud and happy to offer it in the most authoritative translation by renowned translators of Korean literature. We hope that this series helps to build solid bridges between citizens of the world and Koreans through a rich in-depth understanding of Korea.

바이링궐 에디션 한국 대표 소설 075

Bi-lingual Edition Modern Korean Literature 075

What Has Yet to Happen

김미월
아직 일어나지 않은 일

Kim Mi-wol

ASIA
PUBLISHERS

Contents

아직 일어나지 않은 일

What Has Yet to Happen

꿈이었을 거야. 잠에서 깨자마자 생각했다. 정말 이상한 꿈이었어. 머리맡을 더듬어 휴대폰을 찾았다. 오늘 서울의 날씨 맑음. 내일도 맑음. 모레는 흐림. 글피는 다시 맑음. 일기예보 애플리케이션을 종료했다. 여전히 내일이 있고 모레가 있다. 일주일이 있다. 그러니까 아무 일도 일어나지 않은 것이다.

있는 힘껏 기지개를 켰다. 술이 덜 깨서일까. 팔이 내 팔 같지 않고 다리도 내 다리 같지 않은 것이 기지개를 켜도 시원하지가 않았다. 어제 대학 동기 모임에 나간 것은 실로 오랜만이었다. 그중에서 아직 취업을 못한

"It must have been a dream," I think the moment I wake up. "What a strange dream!" I grope for the cell phone at the head of my bed. ***Sunny today in Seoul. Another sunny day tomorrow. Cloudy the day after tomorrow. Back to sunshine the following day.*** I log off the weather forecast application. There's still tomorrow and the day after tomorrow. There's still a whole week ahead. Which means nothing's happened.

I have a good stretch. Am I not fully sober yet? My arms and legs don't feel like my own, and the stretching doesn't help much to ease the numbness. I went to my college class reunion yesterday,

사람은 공과 나 둘뿐이었다. 술자리에 끝까지 남은 것도 우리 둘뿐이었다. 취업 이야기는 하지 않았다. 공은 동생이 저보다 먼저 장가가게 되었다며 투덜거렸고, 나는 결혼 일찍 해봐야 좋을 거 없다며 횡설수설했고, 우리는 서로 술값을 내겠다며 승강이했고, 그리고 어느 틈엔가 각자 집으로 가는 택시를 탔다. 띄엄띄엄이나마 거의 다 기억이 났다. 다만 누가 계산을 했는지를 기억할 수 없었다. 침대에서 몸을 일으켜 탁자 위의 가방으로 팔을 뻗었다. 지퍼를 열자 지갑이 아니라 웬 깡통이 묵직하게 손에 딸려나왔다. 동원 복숭아 황도 400g. 헛웃음이 나왔다. 그것을 괜히 한번 흔들어보았다. 그러나 내 머릿속을 꽉 채운 것은 이게 왜 뜬금없이 내 가방에 들어 있느냐 하는 당혹감이 아니라 어젯밤 꿈이 꿈이라기엔 지나치게 구체적이지 않은가 하는 불안감이었다. 얼마를 더 그렇게 앉아 있었을까. 창밖에서 목소리 굵은 남자가 확성기로 외치는 듯한 소리가 들려왔다. 시민 여러분…… 모두 함께…… 시청 앞 광장으로……

나는 창가로 달려갔다. 건물 삼층에서 내려다보는 토

for the first time in a long time. Kong and I were the only unemployed ones among the classmates. We were also the only ones who stayed behind after the drinking party ended. We didn't talk about jobs. Kong complained about his younger brother getting married ahead of him; I rambled on to the effect that there was nothing great about getting married early. We both insisted on footing the bill. Then, each of us got in a taxi to go home. I remember most of the time I spent with Kong last night except for some blackouts here and there. For instance, I can't remember who settled the bill in the end. I sit up in bed and reach for my purse. I unzip the purse and reach in for my wallet, but, instead of my wallet, my hand emerges with a heavy can tight in my grip. *Tongwon Peach Golden 400 grams.* I'm so taken aback that I can't help laughing to myself. I give the can a useless shake. Oddly enough, what fills my mind at this moment is not the question of how on earth this can's ended up in my purse, but a sense of anxiety; the dream I had last night seems much too concrete and real. Suddenly, I'm startled from my thoughts by a deep male voice, which seems like it's speaking over a megaphone: "Citizens of Seoul... all together... to

요일 오전의 팔차선 대로는 오가는 차량들로 번잡했다. 저만치 육교 밑에서 트럭 한 대가 유난히 느린 속도로 움직이는 것이 보였다. 확성기 소리는 그 트럭에서 흘러나오는 것 같았다.

"그냥 이대로 앉아서 죽을 수는 없습니다!"

"이것은 미국의 거대한 음모입니다, 여러분!"

행인 몇이 걸음을 멈추고 트럭을 향해 고개를 돌렸다가 이내 별일 아니라는 듯 원래 가던 길을 갔다. 트럭 뒤에 있던 승용차가 차선을 바꾸며 경적을 울렸다. 언뜻 보면 여느 주말 아침과 별다를 것 없는 풍경이었다. 하지만 나는 감지할 수 있었다. 거기에 뭔가가 빠져 있다는 것을. 굳이 적당한 단어를 찾는다면 생기라고 부를 수도 있을. 그것이 오늘 아침의 거리에는 없었다.

불현듯 어젯밤 술집 계산대 앞에서 공과 옥신각신하다가 텔레비전 뉴스 속보를 보았던 것이 떠올랐다. 저거 다 뻥이야! 공이 외쳤던가. 맞아, 다 뻥이야! 내가 맞장구쳤던가. 그러고 보니 집에 돌아와 침대에 쓰러지듯 누우면서 했던 생각도 떠올랐다. 자면 안 되는데. 지구가 멸망하는데 잠이 온다니. 말도 안 돼.

the Plaza in front of the City Hall..."

I rush over to the window. Saturday morning traffic on the eight-lane main street from the view of this third floor building looks busy. I spot a truck moving very slowly under an overpass some distance away. The megaphone voice seems to come from the truck.

"We can't just sit and wait for our deaths!"

"Attention, all citizens! This is nothing but a US conspiracy!"

Some passersby stop and turn their heads toward the truck, but continue on their ways shortly after. They seem to think nothing of it. A passenger car behind the truck changes its lanes, honking. At a glance, the street scene is not so different from that of any other weekend morning. And yet I can detect something's missing from the otherwise ordinary view outside. For lack of a better expression, I say there's a vitality that's missing. That's what's absent from this morning street scene.

Without warning, I have a flashback to last night. Kong and I were in front of the counter arguing with each other about the bill when we happened to see a news report on the TV. Probably it was Kong who'd cried, "What a bunch of nonsense!"

정말이지 말도 안 되는 일이었다. 목이 말랐다. 나는 꿈을 꾼 것이 아니었다.

멸망이라고 해야 하나. 아니면 종말이라고 해야 하나. 멸망이든 종말이든 하여간 이 세계가 끝장난단다. 그것도 당장 내일 새벽에.

믿기지 않지만 믿지 않을 도리가 없다고 텔레비전을 보며 나는 생각했다. 광고도 없고, 아침드라마도 없고, 만화영화나 요리 프로그램도 없었다. 모든 채널이 오직 지구 멸망에 대한 특집 뉴스만을 연달아 내보내고 있었다. 어제 심야 뉴스에서 각 방송사가 일제히 외신을 앞세워 긴급 보도한 바에 따르면 태양계 외부의 행성들 중 하나가 지구를 향해 돌진해오고 있다고 했다. 지구와 충돌하기까지 남은 시간은 최초 보도 시각을 기준으로 약 서른 시간. 미 항공우주국을 비롯한 세계 각국의 우주 관련 연구소와 정부 기관이 실시간으로 모든 지구 근접체를 관찰해왔다면서 문제의 행성인지 소행성인지가 지구를 산산조각내기 서른 시간 전에야 그 사실을 세상에 알렸다는 것은 그들이 뭔가를 은폐하고 있을지

And then, hadn't I chimed in, "Right! Nothing but nonsense, right?"

But, come to think of it, as I crashed onto my bed after arriving home, my last thoughts had been, "No, I mustn't fall asleep. The earth is heading toward its doom. How can I sleep? This is absurd."

Absurd indeed! I suddenly feel thirsty. It had not been a dream.

Should I call it the earth's downfall? Or, the end of the earth? Either way, the world as we know it will cease to exist. At dawn tomorrow at that.

It's hard to believe at first, but while watching TV, I can't help turning into a believer. There are no commercials, no morning soap operas, no cartoons, and no cooking shows. All the stations broadcasting the news featuring nothing but the end of the earth. According to last night's late emergency news broadcast, which all stations released simultaneously, citing the foreign news, one of the planets outside the solar system was hurtling toward the earth. About thirty hours were left, counting from the time of the first report, until the planet would make impact.

The space-related research institutes from all

도 모른다는 의혹을 사기 충분했다. 전 지구인이 들고 일어나 음모론 운운하는 것도 당연한 일이었다. 하지만 음모론이라니. 음모를 꾸민 이들도 내일이면 다 죽게 된 마당에 대관절 누구를 위한 무엇을 위한 음모란 말인가.

컴퓨터의 전원을 켰다. 포털사이트도 온통 지구 멸망 관련 기사들뿐이었다. 어떤 기사는 행성이라 하고 어떤 기사는 소행성이라 하는 식으로 세부 정보에 약간의 차이는 있어도 그것이 내일 새벽 지구와 충돌하면 모든 게 끝이라는 결론만큼은 죄 같았다. 나는 문제의 행성을 촬영한 동영상을 재생시켰다. 컴컴한 우주 한가운데 불그스름하게 빛나는 점 같은 것이 하나 찍혀 있었다. 그게 다였다. 그것은 무시무시하지도 않았고 불길하지도 않았다. 천문대에서 나눠주는 달력 사진이나 윈도 바탕화면처럼 근사하지도 않았다. 그것의 반지름이 45마일이고 그것이 현재 지구를 향해 날아오는 속도가 시간당 9백만 마일이라고 내레이터가 설명했지만, 마일이라는 단위에 익숙하지 않으니 그게 얼마나 큰지 얼마나 빠른지 감을 잡을 수도 없었다. 나만 그런 궁금증을

over the world, including NASA, and governments from all over the world had been conducting real-time observation of all the space bodies moving close to the earth. And yet they alerted the rest of the world to the planet, or planetoid in question only thirty hours before it would blow the earth to smithereens. This lapse seemed to provide a solid foundation for the suspicion that they'd been hiding something from the rest of the world. It's only natural that all the citizens from all over the world should be indignant now, accusing these institutes and governments of conspiracy. Nevertheless, the conspiracy theory seems farfetched, given the fact that the alleged conspirators would also die tomorrow with the rest of the world. If it were a conspiracy, then whose interest was it serving?

I turn on the computer. All the portal sites have been plastered with the doomsday news. Some report it as a planet and others as a planetoid. Despite these minor discrepancies, all of them reach the same conclusion: when it collides with the earth tomorrow morning, everything will end. I play back the video of the planet in question. There's a reddish speck shining in the middle of the dark. That's all. It doesn't look grotesque or sinister. Nor

가진 것은 아니었던 듯 과연 인기 검색어에 '1마일은 몇 킬로'가 떠 있었다. 덩달아 에미넴이 출연했던 영화 〈8 마일〉까지 연관 검색어에 올라 있었다. 1마일은 약 1.6 킬로미터였다. 즉 45마일은 대략 72킬로미터, 9백만 마일은 1천4백만 킬로미터가 조금 넘는다고 친절한 네티즌들이 답해주었다. 마일을 킬로미터로 환산해도 감이 잡히지 않기는 마찬가지였다.

인기 검색어는 수시로 바뀌었다. 나사 음모론, 노스트라다무스의 예언, 행성 이름, 행성과 소행성의 차이…… 지구 종말의 순간에도 사람들은 이렇듯 네이버에 묻고 있었다.

휴대폰 벨이 울렸다. 시골집에서 걸려온 전화였다.

"너는 무슨 통화를 그렇게 오래 하냐?"

"저 통화 안 했는데요?"

지구 멸망 하루 전이어서일까. 나도 모르게 존댓말이 나왔다. 어색하게 느껴질 법도 한데 아버지는 그것에 대해서는 아무 말도 하지 않았다.

"그래? 이상하네. 한 시간 전부터 계속 통화 중이던데."

is it as splendid as the pictures in the calendars distributed by the astronomical observatory or the Microsoft Windows' wallpaper design. According to the narrator, it has a radius of 45 miles and is traveling toward the earth at the speed of 9 million miles per hour. I'm not familiar with miles so I've no idea how big it is or how fast it's moving. In fact, I'm not the only one with the problem; one of the most searched phrases I've noticed on search engines over the past day is "How many kilometers is in one mile?" The film "8 Mile" starring Eminem is one of the related search hits. Some Netizens answer that 1 mile is about 1.6 kilometers; 45 miles is some 72 kilometers; and 9 million miles is a little over 1.4 billion kilometers. The conversion doesn't help much. I still have no idea how big and how fast the planet is.

Popular search words keep changing. NASA conspiracy, Nostradamus's prophecy, planet names, difference between planets and planetoids... Even in their final moments on earth, people continue to ask questions on Naver like this.

My cell phone rings. It's my parents from the countryside.

"Goodness, it's so hard to get through to you.

"회선에 문제가 생긴 게 아닐까요. 통신망에 과부하가 걸렸을 수도 있고요."

지금 시국이 비상시국이잖아요 하고 덧붙이려다가 그냥 입을 다물었다.

"테레비 봤냐?"

"네."

"힘든데 니가 내려올 것 없다."

"네?"

"느 엄마 생각도 그렇고. 우리가 서울로 올라가마."

하마터면 왜요 하고 물을 뻔했다. 아버지는 어째서 최후의 날을 가족이 오순도순 모여서 보내야 한다고 생각한 것일까. 평소에 그리 가정적인 사람도 아니었으면서. 그럴 필요 없다고 대꾸하고 싶었다. 하지만 그렇다고 딱히 나 혼자 있고 싶은 것도 아니었다. 그냥 아무 생각이 없었다.

"점심 먹고 바로 출발하면 저녁 전에는 도착할 거다."

"엄마는요?"

"고추 딴다고 밭에 나갔다."

오늘 같은 날 고추를 딴다니. 기가 찼지만 나는 순순

You've been on the phone for ages!"

"I haven't been on the phone all day, Father."

Perhaps, because it's just the day before the catastrophe, I unwittingly speak to my father using the honorific form. Normally, my father would feel awkward about my polite speech but he doesn't say anything about it now.

"Really? That's strange. Your phone's been busy for over an hour."

"I wonder if there's a problem with the circuit. Or, the communication network's overloaded."

I catch myself before I blurt out, "It's an emergency situation, you know."

"Have you watched TV?"

"Yes, Father."

"Don't bother to come all the way down here."

"What'd you mean?"

"Your mother agrees with me. We'll come to Seoul."

I catch myself again before asking him why. What's made him think that the whole family should spend time together in friendly spirits on our last day on the earth? He's never been all that family-oriented. I want to tell him there's no need for that. Not that I want to be alone. I just feel numb inside.

히 네 하고 전화를 끊었다.

어머니는 불쌍한 사람이었다. 하루 종일 집과 밭을 오가며 억척스럽게 일만 했다. 없는 일도 만들어 하고 안 해도 되는 일도 일부러 했다. 누가 시키지도 않는데 도토리를 주워 묵을 쑤고, 감을 말려 곶감을 만들고, 쑥을 캐어 개떡을 빚고, 감자를 갈아 녹말을 내고, 그러고는 과로로 앓아눕는 식이었다. 도대체 왜 그렇게 사느냐 물었더니 일을 하지 않으면 시간이 가지 않는다고 했다. 그러니까 어머니는 놀 줄을 모르는 사람이었던 것이다.

물론 아버지도 알고 보면 불쌍한 사람이었다. 일평생 당신이 태어나고 자란 시골 땅을 벗어나본 적이 없는 그의 유일한 낙은 텔레비전으로 축구 중계를 보는 것이었다. 2002년 한일 월드컵에서 우리나라 대표팀이 4강에 진출하던 때가 인생에서 최고로 행복했던 순간이라고 그는 몇 차례나 진지하게 말했다. 죽기 전에 우리나라가 개최하는 월드컵을 한 번만 더 보는 것이 소원이라고 말하기도 했다. 그의 소원은 이루어지지 않을 것이다.

"We'll leave right after lunch and get there before dinner."

"Where's Mom?"

"Your mom's out in the field picking red peppers."

Harvesting red peppers on a day like this? I'm flabbergasted, but all I can say is "I see," before I hang up.

I feel sorry for my mother. She's spent all her life doggedly working, back and forth between the house and the field. When there's nothing to do, she creates tasks to accomplish for herself, even if there's absolutely no need. She collects acorns to make jelly, dries persimmons, unearths mugworts for rice cakes, grinds potatoes for starch—all only to fall sick in the end from overworking herself. I once asked her why she lived her life that way. She answered, "Time passes painfully slow when you're not working." In a nutshell, my mother doesn't know how to relax and have fun.

Actually, my heart goes out to my father, too. He's never left his country hometown. His only source of joy is watching soccer games on TV. He's told us time and time again, fairly solemnly, the happiest moment of his life was when the Korean na-

아래층에서 피아노 소리가 들렸다. 아니나 다를까, 정각 열한 시였다. 이 건물 이층에는 중년 여자가 운영하는 피아노 교습소가 있었다. 교습 시작 시간은 오후인데 여자는 매일 오전 열한 시면 어김없이 피아노를 쳤다. 매번 같은 곡이었다. 멜로디가 귀에 익숙한데도 나는 번번이 곡명을 떠올리는 데 실패했다. 그런데 저 여자는 오늘 같은 날에도 피아노 칠 기분이 날까. 얼떨결에 멜로디를 따라 흥얼거리다 말고 생각했다. 곡이 끝났다. 열한 시 오 분. 인류 절멸 예정 시각인 내일 새벽 여섯 시까지 약 열아홉 시간 남은 셈이었다. 내 남은 평생 서른 시간 중에서 술 먹고 자는 데 이미 열한 시간을 써버린 것이다. 갑자기 마음이 분주해졌다. 세수부터 해야지 하고 욕실로 들어서다가 순간 멈칫했다. 오늘 같은 날 세수는 무슨 세수.

나는 세수를 했다. 엄마가 고추를 따고 여자가 피아노를 치는 것처럼. 얼굴에 선크림도 발랐다. 내일 지구가 멸망해도 오늘 자외선은 피해야 했으니까. 탁자 위의 황도 통조림이 눈에 들어왔다. 복숭아를 그다지 좋아하지도 않을 뿐더러 통조림이라면 거들떠본 적도 없는데,

tional team made it to the final four during the World Cup co-hosted by Korea and Japan in 2002. He's also said his only wish is to watch another World Cup hosted by Korea before he dies. His wish will never come true.

I hear someone playing the piano downstairs. Sure enough, it's eleven o'clock, on the dot. On the second floor of this building is an apartment where a middle-aged woman gives piano lessons. Lessons begin in the afternoon, but the woman plays the piano at 11 AM everyday without fail. Always the same piece of music. The melody's familiar to me, but I've never been able to recall its title. Unconsciously, I hum along to the music until a question hits me: How on earth is it possible for her to feel like playing the piano on a day like today? The piece ends. Five past eleven. About 19 hours to go till 6 AM tomorrow, the predicted time of humanity's extinction. Of the last 30 hours of my life I've already spent 11 hours drinking and sleeping. Suddenly, thoughts begin swarming my mind. I need to wash up first. Walking into the washroom, I stop in my tracks. Who cares about washing up on a day like this?

But then I wash up anyway. Just like my mother

입 안에 침이 고였다. 탁자로 다가갔다. 애석하게도 원터치 캔이 아니라서 당장 개봉할 수가 없었다. 출처를 모르고 있다는 점도 꺼림칙했다. 공이 술김에 사준 것일까. 혹시 내가 술김에 어디선가 훔친 거라면 어쩌지. 공에게 전화를 걸었다. 두 번 다 통화 중이었다. 통화 중 대기음을 들으면서 나는 배터리가 거의 바닥난 휴대폰을 충전기에 꽂았다. 순간 어찌된 일인지 문자 메시지 예닐곱 통이 한꺼번에 쏟아져 들어왔다.

'그동안 고마웠어. 네가 내 친구여서 행복했다.'

'더 잘해주지 못해서 미안해. 사랑한다, 친구야.'

'하느님이 언니를 지켜주실 거예요. 천국에서 만나요.'

대학 동기며 동아리 후배, 고등학교 때 친구, 사촌동생 등 친한 사람뿐 아니라 평소 안부 주고받는 일이 드물던 이들에게까지 메시지를 받으니 흡사 추석 전날 같은 기분이었다. 메시지 내용은 거개가 비슷했다. 고맙다, 미안하다, 사랑한다…… 어조도 하나같이 진지하고 비장했다. 오직 이동통신사에서 온 메시지만이 밤사이 아무 일도 없었다는 듯 평심을 유지하고 있었다.

'고객님의 금월 무료 통화 시간이 95분 남았습니다.'

picking red peppers and the woman playing the piano downstairs. I put sunscreen on, too. Even if the earth disappears tomorrow, I need to avoid the ultraviolet rays today. The can of peaches on the table comes in sight. Although I don't like peaches and have never paid attention to canned peaches my entire life, my mouth waters now. I walk up to the peaches. Unfortunately, it's not one of those easy-open cans, so I can't open it. The fact that I don't know where it's come from also makes me feel uneasy about eating it. Did Kong buy it for me when he was too drunk to know what he was doing? What if I'd managed to steal them, even as drunk as I was last night? I try to call Kong. His phone's busy even on the second try. As I listen to the busy signal, I insert my cell phone into the charger, noting its battery's almost empty. Suddenly, six or seven text messages pour in one after another.

"Thank you for everything. I'm happy to have had a friend like you."

"I should have paid more attention to you. I'm sorry. I love you, my friend."

"May God be with you, Sister. See you in Heaven."

문득 얼마 전에 24개월 할부로 구입한 스마트폰의 기기 대금을 더 이상 갚지 않아도 되겠구나 하는 생각이 들었다.

배터리를 충전하는 동안에도 카카오톡 메시지들이 속속 도착하는 소리가 요란했다. 나는 메시지를 확인하는 대신 냉장고를 열었다. 이상한 일이었다. 뉴욕의 9·11 테러나 대구 지하철 참사 등 갑작스러운 죽음을 앞두고 사람들이 저마다 소중한 이들에게 전화를 걸어 사랑한다든가 미안하다든가 했다는 일화를 접했을 때와는 느낌이 생판 달랐다. 그때는 남 이야기인데도 슬펐으나 지금은 내 이야기인데도 별 감흥이 없다고 할까. 아마 메시지를 받은 나도 똑같이 죽기 때문일 것이다.

현관문 앞에 서 있는 사람은 우체국 택배기사였다. 그는 삼층까지 뛰어 올라왔는지 숨을 몰아쉬고 있었다.

"이거 옆집 택배인데 좀 맡아주실래요?"

"네? 택배라고요?"

나는 말귀를 한 번에 알아듣고도 내가 제대로 알아들었는지 의심하느라 눈을 끔벅거렸다.

They're from a classmate in college, a junior member of the club I belonged to, a high school friend, a cousin etc. I've been close to some of them. As for the others, however, we've hardly asked after each other, which makes me feel as if it were the eve of Chuseok. The contents of the messages are more or less the same. Thank you, I'm sorry, I love you... Their tones are the same, too: heartfelt and serious. Only the one from my phone company seems composed as if nothing's happened over night:

"Your balance for free-of-charge calls for the month: 95 minutes."

It occurs to me that I don't have to pay for the smartphone that I bought some time ago on a 24-month installment plan.

Even while the battery recharges, new KakaoTalk messages continue to arrive. My phone beeps constantly. Instead of checking the messages, though, I open my refrigerator door. Strange! It feels different from when I first heard of all those people who, in the face of unexpected death, expressed their love or apologies to their beloved over the phone. Like the victims of the September 11th terrorist attack in New York or of the subway

"옆집에 지금 아무도 없는 것 같아서요."

그는 내가 어떤 표정을 짓고 있는지 신경도 쓰지 않았다. 제 손목시계를 흘끔거리고 나서 손등으로 땀이 맺힌 이마를 훔치더니 내 발 앞에 택배 상자를 던지듯 내려놓았다.

"내일 다시 올 순 없으니까, 부탁 좀 할게요."

나는 거절하려고 했다. 옆집 사람과는 말 한마디 나눠본 적 없는 사이이며 나 역시 곧 외출할 예정이라고 말해야 했다. 그러나 그는 이미 돌아서서 걸음을 옮기고 있었다. 땀으로 젖은 그의 등판이 순식간에 계단 아래로 사라져가는 것을 나는 지켜보았다. 맞는 말이었다. 내일 다시 올 수는 없었다. 상자를 현관문 안으로 들여놓았다. 그는 지금 어떤 생각으로 택배를 배달하는 것일까. 직업정신일까. 일종의 사명감 같은 것일까. 상자는 크기에 비해 몹시 가벼웠다. 택배 송장을 살펴보았다. 오늘만 특가, 한방 생리대 6개월분 19,900원. 내일 지구가 멸망하리라는 것을 미리 알았더라면 옆집 여자는 생리대를 한꺼번에 6개월치나 구입하는 짓 같은 것은 하지 않았을 것이다.

arson tragedy in Daegu. On both occasions, I felt very sad even though the victims were complete strangers to me. Now, however, I've no particular feelings even after reading my personal text messages. Perhaps it's because I, the receiver, am about to die along with everyone else.

Standing outside the front door is a deliveryman from the post-office home-delivery service. He's panting as if he's run up the stairs to the third floor.

"This is a home-delivery package addressed to the apartment next to yours. Could you please keep it for your neighbor?"

"Pardon me? Did you say home delivery?"

I understand him but, for some reason, I find myself blinking at him stupidly.

"It seems nobody's home there."

He pays no attention to the look on my face. He takes a glance at his wristwatch and wipes the sweat off his forehead with the back of his hand, before he flops the box down in front of my feet.

"Since I can't come back tomorrow, could you please do me this favor?"

I'm about to refuse, saying I've never spoken to my neighbor and that I'm also on my way out. But

배가 고팠다. 냉장고에는 말라비틀어진 식빵 쪼가리 뿐 요기할 만한 것이 없었다. 찬장에 라면이 있기는 했지만 이 더운 날 그것도 첫 끼니로 라면을 끓여 먹고 싶지는 않았다. 탁자 위의 황도 통조림에 다시금 눈이 갔다. 종말 직전의 묵시록적 풍경 속에 놓인 최후의 식량이 코카콜라도 아니고 깡통에 든 복숭아라니, 뭔가 어설프고 촌스러웠다. 찬장을 열어보았다. 깡통 따개 같은 것이 집에 있을 리 없다는 것은 찬장 앞으로 가기 전부터 알고 있었다. 그래도 나는 온 집 안 수납장을 샅샅이 뒤졌다. 지구에 종말이 오면 마지막으로 하려고 했던 일이 바로 이것이었다는 듯.

그러고 보니 언제였던가, 지구 종말이 하루 앞으로 다가오면 무엇을 할 것인지에 대해 글을 쓴 적이 있었다. 대학 신입생 때였을 것이다. 교양과목 중에 '글쓰기 특강'이라는 수업이 있었다. 막 제대한 복학생이라 해도 믿을 만큼 앳되어 보이던 강사는 대학 강단에 서는 게 처음인지 수업 시간에 어마어마한 양의 유인물을 나눠주고 특이한 과제를 내주는 것으로 자신의 열정과 의욕을 펼쳐보이고는 했다. 유서 쓰기, 소설책 읽고 작가에

the man's already turned around and started to walk away. I just watch his sweat-soaked back disappear down the stairs. He's right. He won't be able to come back tomorrow. I bring the box into the entrance hall. What makes the man still deliver packages at a time like this? Is it his job ethics? A sense of duty? The box is bulky but very light. I examine the invoice: *Today-only special sale, oriental remedy sanitary napkins, quantity six months, 19,900 won*. If my neighbor had known of the earth's imminent death, she would never have purchased this many sanitary napkins at once.

I'm hungry. There's nothing to eat in the refrigerator except for some dried-up slices of bread. I know there's some instant noodles in the cupboard, but I don't want to eat instant noodles on such a hot day, as the first meal of the day to boot. I turn my eyes back to the can of peaches. The last bit of food that's left for me to eat in this apocalyptic scene isn't even a can of Coca-Cola but canned peaches! There is something coarse and unrefined about my situation. I open the cupboard. I know, even before I reached the cupboard, I will never find anything like a can opener in my apartment. Nevertheless, I rummage through all the storage

게 이메일 보내기, 유행가 가사를 바탕으로 이야기 지어내기, 최고의 연애시 찾아오기 등등. 내일 지구가 멸망한다면 무엇을 할 것인지 쓰라는 것도 당시 과제들 중 하나였다.

내일 지구가 멸망한다고 한다. 나는 전부터 짝사랑해 온 남자에게 고백을 하러 가기로 마음먹는다. 그러나 그의 집으로 가려면 버스를 타야 하는데 불행히도 운행 중인 버스가 없다. 버스기사들도 운전대를 팽개치고 각자 사랑하는 이에게 갔기 때문이다. 딱 한 대의 버스만이 정상 운행을 하고 있다. 그 기사는 얼마 전에 실연을 당했고 가족도 없어서 홀로 지구가 멸망하는 순간까지 버스를 몰겠다고 한다. 다만 문제가 있다. 그 버스를 타려는 사람이 너무 많다는 것이다. 누가 버스를 탈 것인지 분란이 일자 기사가 한 가지 제안을 한다. 모두들 자신이 왜 이 버스를 꼭 타야 하는지 이유를 말한 다음 가장 절실한 이유를 가진 사람 순서대로 버스에 태우자는 것이다. 그렇게 하여 이야기 배틀이 펼쳐진다. 참가자들이 사연을 구구절절 이야기하는 동안 해가 지고 밤이 온다. 달이 뜰 무렵 마침내 내 차례가 온다. 나는 내가

closets. As if it were the last task I've always wanted to accomplish when faced with the earth's death.

Suddenly, I'm reminded of an essay I once wrote about what I would do if the earth died the very next day. I was a freshman at university. Among the liberal arts courses offered was "Special Lectures on Writing." The lecturer looked so young that he could have been mistaken for a returnee student fresh out of the army service. It seemed like it was his first course he'd ever taught at a university. He demonstrated his enthusiasm and ambition by preparing reams of handouts for the class and giving unusual assignments: writing a will, reading a novel and sending an e-mail to the writer, creating a story based on the lyrics of a popular song, searching for the best love poem, etc. "What would you do if the earth were to die tomorrow" was one of the assignments at the time.

I've heard that the earth will die tomorrow. I'm determined to visit a man, whom I've loved in secret, and I will confess my love to him. I need to take a bus to get to his place. Unfortunately, though, the buses are not running because the bus drivers have abandoned the wheels and have gone to their beloved ones. After a while, I finally

그 남자를 얼마나 사랑하는지에 대해 이야기하기 시작한다…….

당시 내가 썼던 글의 내용을 나는 아직도 기억하고 있었다. 과제를 제출한 다음 수업 시간에 강사는 나를 호명했다. 강단으로 나와서 과제를 발표하라는 것이었다. 수강생들이 환호성을 지르며 박수를 쳐댔지만 나는 진땀을 흘렸다. 글 뒷부분에서 짝사랑하는 남자에 대한 내 마음을 묘사한 대목을 읽을 때는 말을 더듬기까지 했다. 그도 그럴 것이, 그 남자가 바로 그 강의실에 앉아 있었기 때문이다. 글에 남자의 이름이 등장하지는 않았다. 그래도 그는 알아들었을 거라고 나는 생각했다.

어쨌거나 상상과 현실은 실로 얼마나 판이한 것인가. 지구 종말이 현실로 다가왔건만 나는 짝사랑하는 남자에게 고백하러 가기는커녕, 어디서 났는지도 모를 황도 통조림을 먹기 위해 깡통 따개를 찾아 온 집 안 구석구석을 뒤지고 있었다. 통조림을 노려보았다. 현재 깡통 따개 없이 그것을 먹을 수 있는 방법은 없었다. 그런데도 오기인지 객기인지 꼭 먹어야겠다는 생각이 들었다.

다들 사랑하는 사람을 만나러 가기라도 한 것일까. 이

find a bus, the only one that's still running. The driver's just been dumped and has no family to go to, so he decides to drive the bus until his last moment on the earth. There's one problem, though. Too many people want to get on that bus. Soon great disorder and confusion follows among them. The bus driver makes a suggestion: one by one, they'll tell the driver why they need to take the bus. The driver will then rate them according to the level of seriousness of their reasons and let them get on the bus in that order until the bus is full. The story battle begins. As the people take turns telling their stories, night falls. By the time the moon comes out, it's my turn at last. I begin to tell the driver how much I love a man...

I still remember the story I wrote. In the first lecture after I turned in the assignment, the lecturer called on me to come to the platform and present my assignment to the class. The students in the class hurrahed and applauded, but I had a hell of a time. I even stuttered when I came to the end of the story where the "I" confesses her feelings for the man she's secretly loved. I was very nervous, quite understandably so because the man in my story was sitting right there in that lecture room. I didn't write the man's name in the story. Nonetheless, I believed that he knew whom I was talking

건물 전체에서 내 집 말고 사람이 안에 있는 집은 딱 한 가구밖에 없었다. 여자는 누군지 묻지도 않고 문부터 열어주었다.

"반가워요. 어서 들어와요."

기다리고 있었다는 듯한 여자의 태도에 나는 당황했다.

"아니, 잠깐 뭐 좀 물어보려고요."

여자가 일단 들어와 앉으라고 재촉하는 바람에 엉겁결에 거실 소파에 앉았다. 건물 계단을 오르내릴 때마다 지나쳤으면서도 막상 피아노 교습소 내부에 들어와 보기는 처음이었다. 방 세 칸짜리 가정집을 개조해놓은 실내는 예상보다 넓었다. 거실 한가운데 놓인 그랜드피아노의 위용과 어울리지 않게 깜찍한 뽀로로 매트가 바닥에 깔려 있는 것이 인상적이었다.

여자가 내게 묻지도 않고 아이스커피 두 잔을 내왔다.

"학생이에요?"

"아니요, 취업 준비하고 있어요."

내 입으로 대답해놓고도 취업을 준비하고 있다는 말이 이토록 허무하게 들릴 수 있다는 데 놀랐다. 내일이 없는데 무슨 준비를 한다는 말인가. 정리를 해도 시간

about.

Anyhow, what a difference there is between imagination and reality! The end of the world has become a reality. But, so far, instead of going to the man to confess my love for him, all of I've done is root through every nook and cranny of my apartment for something to open the can with. And I don't even know where the can's come from. I stare at the can. I know I can't eat the peaches without a can opener. And yet, I'm firmly determined to eat them. I don't know if it's bravado or foolhardiness that's taken hold of me.

Have the residents in this building all gone to be with their beloved? There's only one apartment in this entire building, other than mine, that's not empty. The woman opens the door without even asking who it is.

"Nice to meet you. Come on in."

She behaves as if she's been waiting for me, which flusters me quite a bit.

"No, thank you. I just wanted to ask you something."

The woman insists that I come in and have a seat anyway. In spite of myself, I step inside and sit on the couch in her living room. I've always passed by

이 모자랄 판국에. 여자는 내 대답을 들었는지 못 들었는지 표정에 변화가 없었다.

"깡통 따개? 깡통 따는 거? 그건 뭐하려고?"

"복숭아 통조림을 따려고요."

"어쩌지. 그런 건 집에 없는데."

더 이상 할 말이 없었다. 나는 커피를 마셨다. 그동안 커피를 좋아하면서도 신경성 위염 때문에 삼가왔는데 이제는 그럴 필요가 없었다. 여자가 리모컨으로 텔레비전을 켰다. 여전히 지구 멸망을 다룬 특집 프로그램이 이어지고 있었다. 검은색 정장을 차려입은 앵커가 다행히도 밤사이 방화나 약탈, 공공재 파손이나 폭동 등 우려할 만한 범죄는 일어나지 않았다고 했다. 마지막까지 인간으로서의 품위와 질서를 지키려는 고귀한 시민정신의 승리 아니겠느냐고 묻는 목소리가 우스꽝스러울 만큼 비장했다. 여자가 채널을 돌렸다. 화면에 백악관 전경이 비치고 있었다. 거긴 아직 밤이었다. 오바마 대통령이 수많은 카메라 앞에서 열변을 토하는데 화면에 한글 자막이 뜨지 않아서 무슨 말을 하는지 알아들을 수가 없었다. 여자가 다시 채널을 돌렸다. 천체 전문가

the door to this piano studio. I've passed it walking up and down from my apartment. But I've never set foot inside the studio before. It's a three-bedroom family apartment that's been remodeled into a space for piano lessons; and its interior looks more spacious than I expected. In the middle of the living room stands a grand piano on a Little-Penguin-Pororo carpet. The mismatch between the stately grand piano and the cute carpet seems peculiar.

The woman brings out two glasses of iced coffee without even asking me if I care for it.

"Are you a student?"

"No, I'm preparing for employment."

Having said that, I'm startled at the fact that the expression "preparing for employment" can sound so meaningless. What do I prepare for when there's no tomorrow? I don't even have enough time to sort out my life as it is. Whether she's heard me or not, there's no change in the expression on her face.

"A can opener? You mean the thing you open cans with? What do you need that for?"

"I want to open a can of peaches."

"I'm sorry, but I don't keep things like that here."

I've nothing else to say to her. I just drink the

입네 과학자입네 하는 이들이 어떻게 갑자기 이런 일이 벌어졌는지 토론하고 있었다. 행성이 블랙홀과 충돌하여 궤도를 이탈했다는 둥 태양 폭발이 행성의 이동 경로에 영향을 미쳤다는 둥 요령부득의 설전을 보다가 내가 여자를 향해 물었다.

"지구가 멸망한다는 거…… 정말일까요?"

"그렇겠지요. 텔레비전에서 정말이라고 하는데."

나는 고개를 끄덕였다. 우리는 다시 텔레비전으로 시선을 돌렸다. 정말일까. 정말 내일 지구가 멸망할까. 그 진위를 판단하기 위해 우리가 할 수 있는 일은 그저 이렇게 텔레비전을 보는 것밖에 없었다. 하기야 어떤 진실은 너무 거대해서 오히려 이렇게 작은 화면으로밖에 확인할 수 없을 것이다.

여자가 한숨을 쉬었다. 마지막 날인데 할 일도 없고 갈 데도 없다고 했다. 시집 간 딸은 자기 가족과 함께 시간을 보내기로 했고, 종교에 미친 남편은 휴거를 준비한다며 신도들과 어울려 산으로 올라갔다는 것이었다. 내일 지구가 멸망하지 않는다면 오늘 처음 인사를 나눈 위층집 처녀에게 결코 하지 않을 종류의 이야기였다.

coffee. I like coffee, but because of my neuro-gastritis, I've kept myself off it. Now, however, there's no need for the precaution. The woman turns on the television using the remote control. The program featuring the end of the earth is still on. An anchorman in a black suit announces that fortunately there have been no major crimes—such as arson, looting, vandalism, riots, etc.—that have been reported overnight. He asks a rhetorical question: Is this not the triumph of the noble civic spirit, possessed by law-abiding citizens everywhere, striving to keep human dignity intact? His voice sounds tragic to the point of being ridiculous.

The woman changes the channel. Now, a panoramic view of the White House appears on screen. It's still night over there. President Obama is delivering a fervent speech in front of countless cameras. But there are no Korean captions and so I can't understand what he's saying. The woman changes the channel again. This time, the so-called experts and scientists in astronomy are debating how a catastrophe like this can occur so unexpectedly. One theory is that the planet has collided with a black hole and veered away from its orbit. An-

나는 자리에서 일어났다.

"저는 그만 가볼게요."

"그래요."

여자가 별안간 나를 가볍게 끌어안았다 놓았다. 어처구니없는 포옹이었지만 지금 헤어지면 다시는 못 보겠거니 생각하자 나까지 어처구니없게 목이 메려고 했다. 등 뒤에서 교습소의 문이 닫혔다. 그제야 아침마다 여자가 연주하던 피아노곡의 제목을 물어보지 않았다는 것이 떠올랐다. 상관없었다. 다 부질없었다. 이제 와서 곡명을 안들 무엇하랴.

그러니까 내일 지구가 멸망한다는 건 그런 것이었다. 내일 죽는다는 게 문제가 아니라, 죽기 전까지 매 순간 모든 생각 모든 행동이 부질없어진다는 것이 문제였다. 아직 살아 있는데도 세상에 의미 있는 일이 하나도 없다는 것, 그게 죽는 것보다 더 무서운 일이었다.

앵커가 말한 그대로였다. 거리는 여느 때와 크게 다르지 않았다. 지하철도 버스도 모두 정상적으로 운행되고 있었다. 보행자들은 횡단보도 앞에 서서 신호등에 파란

other theorizes that a solar flare has affected the planet's original course of travel. While listening to their pointless verbal battle, I ask the woman:

"The end of the world... Is it really gonna happen?"

"I guess so. They say on TV it's real, so..."

I nod and say no more. We turned our eyes back to the TV screen. Is it true? Is the earth really going to meet its end tomorrow? All we can do to confirm if it's true or not is watch TV like this. Arguably, some truths are so colossal that we can only confirm them via something small like a television screen.

The woman sighs: she has nothing to do and no place to go on the last day of her life. Her married daughter's decided to stay with her own family; and her fanatic husband's gone up a mountain with other believers to prepare for the "rapture." If the earth were not going to end tomorrow, she never would have told all of this to me, a young woman living upstairs whom she'd met for the first time today. I get up to leave.

"I'm afraid I have to leave now."

She says okay and then, without warning, gives me a brief hug. It's completely absurd for her to

불이 켜지면 걷고 빨간불이 켜지면 멈추었다. 간혹 정지 신호를 무시하고 달리거나 불법 유턴을 하는 승용차들이 눈에 띄었지만 그건 지구 종말이 아니어도 흔히 있는 일들이었다.

물론 색다른 풍경이 있기는 했다. 대형할인마트는 주말 대목인데 출입구를 아예 봉쇄해버렸다. 그와 대조적으로 소규모 슈퍼마켓들은 필요한 물건이 있으면 가져가라는 안내문을 출입문에 붙여놓았다. 행인들에게 갓 구운 빵을 나눠주는 빵집이 있는가 하면 아이스크림을 그냥 퍼주는 아이스크림 전문점도 있었다. 노숙자 행색을 한 사내 둘이 편의점 파라솔 아래 마주앉아 소주를 박스째 쌓아놓고 마시는 모습은 심지어 평화로워 보이기까지 했다. 지구 종말을 다룬 영화에서처럼 묻지마 살인이라든가 강간, 방화, 죄수들의 집단 탈옥, 폭탄 테러 같은 극적인 사건들은 일어나지 않았다. 아마도 그 모든 게 부질없기 때문일 거라고 나는 생각했다. 어차피 내일이면 다 끝난다는 체념이 일체의 욕망과 행동 의지를 지배하기 때문이리라고 말이다.

오늘따라 종로 방면으로 가는 버스가 좀처럼 오지 않

give me a hug, but what's more absurd is the fact that I almost feel a lump in my throat thinking that I'll never be able to see her again. The door closes behind me. Only now do I realize that I've forgotten to find out the title of the piano music she's played every morning. It doesn't matter. Nothing matters. What's the use of learning the name of the song now?

That's what it's like to know that the earth will end tomorrow. The problem isn't the fact that I'll die tomorrow but the sense of futility I feel about every thought I own and everything I'll do until the moment of my death. I'm still alive, and yet nothing in the world is meaningful to me anymore. That's what scares me more than my death itself.

As the anchorman has said, streets don't look very different from usual. Subway trains and buses are all running on schedule. At crosswalks, pedestrians stop at the red light and walk at the green. Now and then, I see a car run the red light or make an illegal U-turn, but there have always been drivers like that, regardless of the pending doomsday.

Of course, I see some new scenes added to the otherwise ordinary streets. Large-scale discount

왔다. 버스 도착 안내 전광판을 보려고 몸을 돌리자 얇은 천가방 안의 황도 통조림이 옆구리를 쳤다. 이게 어젯밤 공이 먹고 싶어서 일부러 산 것이었다니.

공과 통화가 되었을 때만 해도 그를 만날 계획은 없었다. 그는 대뜸 무엇을 어떻게 해야 할지 모르겠다고 했다. 주말이면 으레 취업 준비 스터디에 갔다가 독서실로 직행하는데 오늘은 그럴 수 없었으니까. 엊그제 환갑 기념으로 부부 동반 제주도 여행을 떠난 부모님은 오늘 아침 그에게 전화를 걸어 항공권을 구할 수가 없다며 울부짖었고, 동생은 조금 전까지 망연자실해 있다가 결국 죽기 전에 둘이서라도 결혼식을 치르겠다며 애인에게 달려갔다고 했다. 속 쓰리고 배도 고픈데 설상가상으로 황도 통조림을 어딘가에 흘리고 온 것 같다는 공의 말에 나는 소스라쳤다. 그것이 내게 있노라 털어놓으면서도 설마 돌려달라고 하진 않겠지 싶었는데 그가 당장 시간과 장소를 정하라고 했다. 통조림도 받을 겸 죽기 전에 해장도 할 겸 만나자는 것이었다.

버스가 왔다. 승차 단말기에 교통카드를 대려고 하자 운전기사가 말했다.

stores have blocked up their entrances and exits, even though it's their weekend rush period. In contrast to them, small-scale supermarkets have put up a sign on their entrance doors asking people to take whatever they need free of charge. Some bakeries are dispensing free bread to the passersby. There are ice-cream parlors following suit. Two men, homeless by the looks of their outfits, are drinking *soju,* sitting at a table under a beach parasol outside a convenience store. There are boxes of *soju* bottles stacked up beside the table. I might even say the scene as peaceful. Unlike in doomsday movies, there haven't been any dramatic events like random murders, rapes, arson, mass prison breakouts, and terrorist bombing. Probably because all of this would be futile, too, I think. People are resigned to the fact that everything will be over tomorrow anyway, and their resignation controls their desire and behavioral volition.

It's high time that one of the Jongno-bound buses arrived at the bus stop; they're strangely rare today. When I turn around to check the bus schedule on the electric screen, the can of peaches in my cloth purse pokes me in the side. I can't believe

"그냥 타세요."

그는 나 다음으로 버스에 오르는 이들에게도 같은 말을 반복했다. 그래도 꿋꿋하게 카드를 가져다대는 승객들이 있었다. 그럴 때면 운전석 바로 뒷자리에 앉은 깡마른 노인이 기사 대신 나서서 참견을 했다.

"에헤이, 오늘은 다 공짜라니까!"

버스가 출발하자 노인은 좌석에 앉은 채 상체를 뒤로 틀어 승객들에게 외쳤다.

"예수 믿고 구원받으세요! 안 그러면 지옥 갑니다!"

기사가 운전에 방해된다며 조용히 해달라고 했다. 노인은 의외로 금방 입을 다물었다. 승객들 가운데 누구 하나 말을 하는 사람이 없었다. 버스 안이 너무 조용해서 마치 종로가 아니라 저승 가는 버스에 타고 있는 것 같았다. 기사가 라디오를 틀었다. 당연히 지구 종말 관련 뉴스가 나올 줄 알았는데 음악이 흘러나오다 멎었다.

"오늘은 특별히 두 시간 내내 청취자 여러분의 신청곡과 함께할게요."

디제이의 목소리가 귀에 익었다. 섹스 비디오 유출 파문으로 한때 연예계에서 퇴출당하다시피 했던 여자 가

that Kong bought it last night when he felt like eating canned peaches.

Even when I finally got Kong on the phone, I had no plans to meet him. The first thing he said was he didn't know what to do. His usual weekend schedule's simple: go to the employment preparation study center and then on to the reading room. But today he said he just couldn't do it. The day before yesterday, his parents went on a trip to Jeju Island to celebrate their 60th birthday there. This morning, they cried over the phone saying that they couldn't get the plane tickets to return home. His younger brother, who'd been utterly stupefied, finally arrived at his lover's just a few minutes before, determined to get married while they were still alive, even if no one else could come to their wedding. Kong said his stomach burned and he was hungry, then he added that to make it worse, he seemed to have lost his can of peaches somewhere. I was shocked. As I told him that I had the can with me I felt pretty sure that he wouldn't ask me to return it. But I was wrong. He immediately asked me to set the time and place to meet him. He wanted to meet me not only to get the can back but also to take care of his hangover before

수였다. 이번에 재기하면서 라디오 가요프로그램의 디제이를 맡았다는 기사를 어디선가 읽은 기억이 났다. 그런데 그녀의 이름이 기억나지 않았다. 휴대폰으로 검색해볼까 하다가 그만두었다. 다 부질없는 짓이었다. 차창 밖으로 눈길을 주었다. 광화문에서 종로 방향으로 차가 몹시 막혔다. 전경 버스 수십 대가 광화문 광장을 둘러싸고 있었다.

"백 퍼센트 틀어드린다니까요? 음악 좀 신청해주세요, 네?"

디제이의 말투는 애원에 가까웠다.

"지금 라디오 듣고 계시죠? 전화나 문자로 신청곡 올려주세요."

하긴 누가 오늘 같은 날 라디오를 들으며 음악을 신청하겠는가. 교통 체증이 점점 심해졌다. 종로가 코앞인데 이 상태로 계속 가다가는 약속 시간에 늦을지도 몰랐다.

"청취자 여러분, 그거 아세요? 인류가 완전히 멸종한 후에도, 모든 문명이 완벽하게 사라진 후에도, 인간이 남긴 텔레비전과 라디오 방송의 전파는 영원히 우주를

he died.

The bus arrives at last. As I'm about to place my transit card on the boarding monitor the driver says:

"No need for that."

The driver repeats the same phrase to all the other passengers behind me. Still, some passengers insist on using their transit cards. Each time, a lean, old man sitting right behind the driver's seat butts in on behalf of the driver.

"Come on, everything's free today!"

When the bus begins to move again, the old man turns his upper body from his sitting position and shouts to the other passengers:

"Trust in God, and you'll be saved! Or, you'll go to hell!"

The bus driver tells the old man to be quiet so as not to distract him from driving. Unexpectedly, the old man clams up right away. Now, all the passengers remain silent. It's so quiet inside the bus that I feel as if I were on a bus bound not for Jongno, but for the world of the dead. The driver switches the radio on. I expect to hear news about the end of the world but music flows out briefly and then stops.

떠돌아다닌다고 합니다. 그러니까 지금 제가 틀어드리는 노래, 지금 제가 하고 있는 멘트, 이것들은 사라지지 않는다는 거예요. 영원히, 영원히 우주를 떠도는……"

디제이가 말끝을 흐렸다. 잠시 흐느끼는 소리가 나더니 설마 하는 사이 통곡으로 이어졌다. 방송 사고였다. 마이크가 뭔가에 부딪치는 듯한 소음이 나고 곧바로 음악이 흘러나왔다. 모든 인류가 세상을 떠난 후에도 언제까지나 영원히 이 우주를 떠돌아다닐 음악이.

나는 광화문 정류장에서 하차했다. 종각역까지 걸어가는 게 더 빠를 것 같았다. 광화문 광장을 가로지르는데 사람들이 한곳에 모여 있는 것이 보였다. 세종대왕 동상 앞에서 한 남자가 고통 없이 죽을 수 있다는 드링크제를 팔고 있었다.

"한 병에 만 원! 고통 없는 죽음이 단돈 만 원!"

죽을 때 고통스러울지 어떨지 그것까지는 생각해보지 않았는데, 남자는 내일 죽기 직전에 이 음료를 마시면 잠자는 듯 평화롭게 죽을 수 있다고 했다. 좌판에는 박카스병에서 스티커만 떼어낸 것처럼 보이는 갈색 병들이 진열되어 있었다. 구경하던 사람들 중에서 누군가

"For one day only, we have a special offer for all our listeners. For two solid hours, I'll play nothing but the songs requested by the audience."

The voice of the DJ sounds familiar. It's the woman singer who was once almost expelled from the entertainment industry for the sensation she'd caused by the pornographic video she'd starred in. I remember reading an article somewhere that she'd made a comeback and had become a DJ for a folk music radio program. I can't remember her name. I consider using my cellphone and looking her up on the Internet. But, I decide not to. It's all vain. I look out the window. There's a terrible traffic jam stretching from Gwanghwamun to Jongno. Dozens of the riot-police buses surround the Gwanghwamun Plaza.

"I promise I'll play all of your requests! Make a request now. Could you—please?"

She sounds like she's almost pleading.

"You're listening to the radio, aren't you? Either by phone or by text message, please."

In fact, who on earth would listen to the radio and request a song on a day like this? The traffic jam's getting worse. Jongno's right around the corner. But if I stay on this bus, I may be late for the

소리쳤다.

"그냥 나눠주지, 뭘 팔아? 인제 돈 벌어서 어디다 쓰게?"

"아따, 뭘 모르는 말씀이십니다. 저승길에서도 노자는 필요하지요."

남자는 약장수답게 언변이 좋았다. 중절모를 쓴 노인이 좌판 앞에 쪼그려 앉더니 약병을 햇빛에 비춰가며 요리조리 돌려보았다.

"이게 뭘로 만들어진 거요?"

"어르신, 제가 설마 오늘 같은 날 몸에 나쁜 걸 팔겠습니까?"

남자는 고대 중국 황실에서부터 전해 내려온 신비의 명약이 어쩌고 불로장생의 비밀이 저쩌고 하면서 끝까지 성분을 말해주지 않았다.

"그거 한 병만 주세요."

선뜻 지갑을 연 사람은 나였다. 모여 있던 사람들이 동시에 나를 쳐다보았다. 고통 없이 죽고 싶어서가 아니었다. 어차피 죽는데 고통이 있으면 어떻고 없으면 또 어떤가. 나는 그냥 뭔가를 사보고 싶었다. 아직도 화

appointment.

"Dear audience, you know what? Even after the extinction of the human race, after the entire civilized world disappears, the television and radio sound waves left by humans will float through space forever. So, the songs I'm playing and the remarks I'm making now will never disappear. They'll remain forever and ever, drifting through the universe..."

The voice of the DJ trails off. Then I hear her sobbing, which quickly turns into a wailing. It's a broadcast mishap. Next comes a noise like a microphone bumping into something, and then music follows immediately. The music that will drift around the space forever and ever, even after the entire mankind dies out.

I get off at Gwanghwamun. It'll be faster to walk to the Jonggak subway station. Crossing the Gwanghwamun Plaza, I catch sight of a crowd gathered around something. In front of the statue of Sejong the Great, a man's selling some sort of elixir that's supposed to help people die without pain.

"Ten-thousand *won* a bottle! Only ten-thousand *won* for a painless death."

폐가 통용되는지 확인해보고 싶었다고 할까. 물건을 사는 이가 나타나니 도리어 구경할 맛이 반감되었는지 사람들이 하나둘씩 자리를 떴다. 이윽고 좌판 앞에는 나 혼자 남았다.

"아저씨, 이거 성분이 뭐예요?"

"응, 이거? 그냥 박카스야."

남자는 목소리를 낮추지도 않았다. 물건을 산 사람이니까 특별히 말해주는 거라며 허허 웃기까지 했다. 결국은 사기였다. 그는 사기꾼이었다. 그런데도 나는 화가 나지 않았다.

"그런데 돈은 받아서 뭐하시려고요? 어차피 못 쓸 텐데."

"훙, 난 절대 안 속아."

"네?"

그는 내일 지구가 멸망한다는 것을 믿지 않는다고 했다. 신문 기사도 텔레비전 뉴스도 전부 날조된 것이라고 했다. 멀쩡한 세상이 어떻게 하루아침에 사라질 수가 있느냐는 것이었다. 하다못해 비가 오기 전에는 먹구름이 끼고 임신하기 전에는 태몽을 꾸게 마련인데,

I haven't been worried about the pain of death yet. According to the man, if we drink that potion just before we die tomorrow, we'll have a peaceful death. Just like falling asleep. On the display mat brown bottles that look just like Bacchus soft drinks are splayed out, only their labels removed. One of the onlookers shouts:

"Why don't you just give them away free? Why're you selling them? What are you going to use the money for?"

"My, you really don't know, do you? I need money to travel to the land of the dead."

The man's as glib as any silver-tongued salesman. One elderly man in a soft hat squats on his haunches beside the display mat and examines a bottle carefully. He holds it up against sunlight.

"What's it made from?"

"Sir, do you really think I would sell something unhealthy on a day like today?"

The man continues to talk about some mysterious elixir handed down from the ancient Chinese royal family blah blah blah and the secret of eternal youth and longevity blah blah blah but refuses to reveal the bottle's ingredients.

"I'll take one."

아무 징조도 없이 지구가 통째로 사라질 수는 없다고 그는 말했다.

정말 아무 징조도 없었을까. 아니, 있었다 한들 내가 알아차릴 수는 있었을까.

종각역을 향해 걸었다. 공은 삼십 분쯤 늦을 거라고 했다. 승용차를 끌고 나왔는데 종로 거의 다 와서 길이 막혀 오도 가도 못하고 있다는 것이었다. 나는 혹시나 하는 마음에 부모님께 전화를 걸어보았다. 아버지는 집에서 출발한 지 두 시간이 넘었는데 고속도로에 들어선 후로 정체가 심해 꼼짝달싹 못하고 있다고 했다. 전국 어디나 도로 사정이 마찬가지인 모양이었다.

"천천히 오세요."

"빨리 가야지, 그게 무슨 소리냐."

"아……"

생각해보니 우리에게는 시간이 없었다. 내일 지구가 멸망한다는 거대한 사실을 실감하게 되는 것은 의외로 이렇게나 작고 보잘것없는 순간들이었다. 보신각 앞에 다다랐다. 인도 곳곳에 오늘자 조간신문이 무더기로 쌓

I'm the one who's willing to open the purse. All eyes are focused on me at once. It's not that I want a painless death. I'll die anyway, so what difference does it make if I die with or without pain? I just wanted to try buying something. In other words, I wanted to find out if the currency was still good. Perhaps my purchase has dashed the spectators' curiosity because they begin to walk away one after another. In the end, I'm the only one who remains by the display mat.

"Mister, what's this made from?"

"This? It's just Bacchus."

The man doesn't even try to lower his voice. I'm told the truth as a bonus since I've bought his product. He's laughing. It's all a scam after all. He's nothing but a con man. Even so, I can't muster any anger.

"But then, why did you take the money? You won't be able to spend it anyway."

"Humph! No one can fool me."

"What'd you mean?"

He says he doesn't believe that the earth will end tomorrow. All the newspaper articles and TV news, he continues, have been made up. How can the world, with which one finds nothing out of the or-

여 있는 것이 보였다. 그중에는 어젯밤 긴급 뉴스가 터지기 전에 발행한 것인지 일면 중앙에 '초복 특수에도 닭고기값 폭락' 기사가 실린 일간지도 있었다.

징조가 있었을지도 모른다. 그러나 징조가 징조였음을 깨닫게 되는 것은 대개 사건이 터진 후다. 아무 사건도 일어나지 않았다면 그것이 징조인 줄도 몰랐을 사소한 징조들. 나는 가을에 있을 중등교사 임용시험을 준비하고 있었고, 동네 보습학원에서 중등반 수학 강사 아르바이트를 하고 있었다. 어쩌다 가끔 친구들을 만나 술을 마셨고, 인터넷에서 인기 영화를 다운로드해 보았으며, 한 달에 한 번꼴로 부모님이 계신 시골에 다녀왔다. 특별한 일이라고는 없었다. 어젯밤 오랜만에 대학 동기 모임에 나간 것이 문제였을까. 마시지도 못하는 술을 넙죽넙죽 받아 마신 게 징조였을까. 아무리 생각해도 모를 일이었다.

공이 도착한 것은 세 시를 훌쩍 넘긴 때였다. 그는 태어나서 이 정도로 극심한 교통 정체는 처음 겪는다고 했다. 시내 중심가를 따라 전경 버스가 끝없이 늘어서 있고 도로 한가운데 버려지는 차가 점점 많아지고 있으

dinary, suddenly disappear overnight? Before the rain comes the dark clouds; before conception comes the precognitive dream of the baby's birth. So, he concludes, it isn't possible for the entire earth to disappear without any omens.

Have there been no omens? Even if I had seen any, could I have recognized it as *the* omen?

I walk toward the Jonggak subway station. Kong's told me that he's going to be about half an hour late. He's in his car stuck in a terrible traffic jam near Jongno. I call my parents just in case. My father says they left home over two hours ago, but they're also stuck in traffic on the expressway. The traffic situation seems to be the same all across the country.

"Take your time, Father."

"What're you talking about? We've got to hurry."

"Ah..."

Come to think of it, we don't have much time left. Ironically, it's only through trivial problems like these that the colossal notion of the impending end of the world comes home to me. I arrive at the Boshin Bell Pavilion. Here and there along the sidewalk are piles of today's morning papers. One

니 상황이 더욱 악화될 거라고도 했다.

"버려지는 차라니?"

"길이 너무 막히니까 다들 도로에 차를 버리고 걸어 가는 거지."

껌은 껌종이에 싸서 버리는 거지 하고 말하는 것처럼 심드렁한 어조였다. 공이 앞장서서 단골 해장국집 쪽으로 걸었다.

"그런데 참, 니 차는 어디다 뒀어?"

"나도 버리고 왔어."

그는 씩 웃었지만 나는 따라 웃을 수가 없었다. 자동차를 버리다니, 그런 일은 재난 영화에서나 가능한 줄 알았는데. 과연 종각에서 동대문 방면으로 차량 행렬이 길게 이어졌다. 다들 어디로 가는 것일까. 가족을 만나러 가는 것일까. 애인을 만나러 가는 것일까. 저들 속에 내 부모님도 끼어 있겠거니 생각하자 마음이 무거웠다. 멈춰 서 있던 자동차들 사이를 오토바이 수십 대가 굉음과 함께 지그재그 곡예를 부리며 보란 듯이 빠져나갔다.

종각역 뒤편 해장국집의 문은 닫혀 있었다. 우리는 마침 근처 떡집에서 나눠주는 떡을 먹으며 발 닿는 대로

of them, which seems to have been printed before the last night's emergency news release, is a daily with the headline "Chicken Price Plummets Despite Special Procurement of Dog Days" at the center of the front page.

There may have been some signs. However, it's usually after the event that people come to realize they were in fact the signs—the trivial signs that one wouldn't have recognized as signs if nothing had happened. I've been preparing for the secondary-school teachers employment exam scheduled for the fall, and teaching an intermediate-level class at a neighborhood private academy as a part-time math teacher. I sometimes met my friends for a drink, watched popular movies I'd downloaded from the Internet other times, and visited my parents in the country roughly once a month. Nothing unusual had happened. I went to the class reunion last night for the first time in a long while. Was that a sign? Although I'm not much of a drinker, I kept emptying glass after glass as my old classmates kept filling them for me. Was that an omen? I'm still in the dark, no matter how hard I search for the answer.

Kong arrives long after three. He complains that

걸었다. 땅만 보고 걷는데 공이 내 어깨를 쳤다. 거리의 행인들이 모두 고개를 쳐들고 있는 것이 눈에 들어왔다. 그들의 시선을 따라간 곳에 이명박 대통령이 있었다. 그러니까 광화문 사거리 빌딩들의 대형 전광판에 하나같이 이명박 대통령의 얼굴이 비치고 있었다. 대국민 연설을 시작하겠다는 안내 방송이 흘러나왔다.

"존경하는 국민 여러분."

스피커가 어디에 있는지 몰라도 목소리가 머리 위에서 들려오니 꼭 그가 벌써 하늘나라에 가 있는 것 같았다. 우리는 걸음을 멈추었다. 사실 지구 멸망 전날 일국의 대통령이 국민들에게 할 이야기란 새해 아침 아나운서들이 다사다난했던 한 해가 가고 운운하는 멘트처럼 뻔할 것이다. 그럼에도 나는 그가 서울 시장이었던 시절 전과가 있는 만큼 이번에는 지구를 하느님께 바친다고 하면 어쩌나 걱정이었다.

대통령은 차분하게 말을 이었다. 본인은 대한민국 국민으로서 언제나 자랑스러웠고…… 국민 여러분을 존경하고 사랑하며…… 어떤 고난과 역경 속에서도 당당하게…… 그가 갑자기 손수건을 꺼냈다.

he's never experienced so severe a traffic jam in his entire life. According to him, the riot-police buses had all lined the downtown streets; the growing number of abandoned cars would only make the situation worse.

"Abandoned cars?"

"Yeah, the traffic jam's much too severe, so the drivers leave their cars right there and walk to their destinations."

Kong sounds so indifferent, as if he were saying something like, "You should wrap chewing gum in the wrapper before you throw it away." He walks ahead of me toward the *haejang* stew restaurant he frequents to chase his hangovers.

"By the way, where's your car?"

"I ditched it, too."

He smiles, but I can't smile along. Ditch a car? I'd thought that kind of thing happened only in the disaster movies. Indeed, there are long lines of cars stretching from Jonggak toward Dongdaemun. Where are they all going? Are they going to see their families? Their lovers? I get heavy-hearted thinking that my parents must be in one of those cars. Skillfully zigzagging through the idling cars, dozens of motorcycles escape the jam, smug and

"국민 여러분, 정말 죄송합니다."

손수건으로 눈가를 찍는 품이 아무래도 눈물을 흘리는 것 같았다. 눈물이야 흘릴 수 있지만 지구가 멸망하는 것은 그의 잘못이 아니었다. 그가 죄송해할 필요는 없었다. 등 뒤에서 자동차들이 경적을 울려댔다. 어느 틈엔가 광화문 우체국 앞 도로에도 운전자가 버리고 간 차들이 하나둘 생기고 있었다. 어디서 나타났는지 속옷 차림의 젊은 여자가 도로 한가운데로 뛰어들었다. 차 안에 있던 사람들이 휴대폰을 꺼내 여자의 사진을 찍었다. 전경들이 여자의 팔을 잡고 도로에서 끌어내려 하자 여자가 발버둥을 치며 울음을 터뜨렸다. 아수라장이 된 도로 위를 한 소년이 스케이트보드를 타고 지나갔다.

걷다보니 시청 방향이었다. 더웠다. 다리도 아팠다. 우리는 청계천 근처 공원의 벤치에 앉았다. 공이 휴대폰을 들여다보더니 사람들이 지금 시청 앞 광장으로 몰려가고 있다고 했다. 트위터 사용자들이 모두 함께 시청 앞 광장으로 모이자는 메시지를 사방으로 퍼 나르고 있다는 것이었다.

"시청 광장에 모여서 뭘 하려고?"

noisy.

The restaurant behind the Jonggak station is closed. We receive free rice cake at the nearby bakery. We eat the cake and wander aimlessly wherever our steps lead us. As I walk with my head bowed, Kong pats me on the shoulder. Then I see all the people in the street looking up at something. At the far end of their line of sight is President Myung-bak Lee. All of the large-screens on the tall buildings around the Gwanghwamun intersection show the face of President Lee Myung-bak. And then the speakers make an announcement that the president will now address all the citizens of Korea.

"My revered citizens."

I don't know where the speaker is, but his voice coming from far above gives me an impression that he's already in Heaven. We stop there. In fact, a presidential address one day before the earth collapses seems a little too crass and obvious, like the hackneyed announcement of an anchor on New Year's Day. This has been an eventful year blah blah blah. Despite it all, I'm worried since he's set a precedent for saying improper things when he was the mayor of Seoul. Who knows? He may offer the

"글쎄. 아무것도 안 하고 죽긴 좀 억울하니까."

그는 이렇게 될 줄 알았으면 취업 준비 같은 건 진작 때려치우고 여행이나 다니는 건데, 여자들이랑 섹스나 실컷 해보는 건데, 하더니 불쑥 물었다.

"지금 세상에서 제일 억울한 사람이 누군지 알아?"

"음…… 부자?"

"내일 치아 교정 끝내는 사람."

나는 소리 내어 웃었다. 그는 계속 주워섬겼다. 내일 제대하는 군인, 내일 대학에 합격하는 수험생, 내일 내 집 마련하는 가장, 내일 아기를 낳는 임부, 내일 태어나는 아기…… 가장 억울한 사람은 현재 가진 게 많은 사람이 아니라 기다릴 미래가 있는 사람이었다.

"핼리혜성 말이야."

"응?"

공이 먼 하늘을 쳐다보았다.

"지구가 멸망한 후에도 핼리혜성이 찾아올까?"

그는 약 76년을 주기로 지구를 지나가는 핼리혜성이 1986년에 관찰되었으니까 계산대로라면 2062년에 다시 올 것이라고 했다. 어렸을 때부터 2062년 팔십 노인

earth to God this time.

The president continues calmly: "I've always been proud to be a citizen of the Republic of Korea... I respect and love the citizens of my country... undaunted in the face of any hardships and adversities..." He suddenly pulls out his handkerchief.

"My dear citizens, I'm truly sorry."

Judging by the way he dabs his eyes with the handkerchief, he must be crying for real. His tears may be sincere, but the end of the world isn't really his fault. There's no need for him to apologize. From behind my back, drivers start to honk. Driver after driver abandons their cars right there on the road in front of the Gwanghwamun Post Office, too. Out of nowhere, a young woman, wearing only her underwear, dashes into the center of the road. The people still in their cars pull out their cell phones and begin to take pictures of the woman. Some riot policemen manage to catch her and hold her by the arms and attempt to drag her out of the road. But she bursts into tears, kicking and struggling. A boy on a skateboard flies across the absurd scene.

We find ourselves walking toward the City Hall. It's so hot. Our legs hurt. We sit down on one of the

이 된 자신이 그것을 직접 보는 순간을 늘 상상해왔는데, 정작 핼리혜성이 다가올 때 자신은 지구에 없으리라는 것이 억울하다고 했다.

나는 대꾸 없이 휴대폰을 들여다보았다. 우리가 사라지고 난 후의 세상에 대한 이야기라니, 상상이 가지 않았다. 우리가 사라지는 순간도 상상이 가지 않는데. 믿을 수조차 없는데. 어느새 오후 네 시였다. 문득 궁금했다. 공은 기억하고 있을까. 오래전 대학 교양 수업 시간에 우리가 지구 멸망에 관한 작문 과제를 했던 것을, 그때 내가 발표했던 글의 내용을. 그는 알아들었을까.

"몇 시간 남았냐?"

"음, 열네 시간 정도?"

휴대폰을 가방에 넣었다. 그리고 황도 통조림을 꺼냈다. 실은 먹으려고 했는데 깡통 따개가 없어서 못 먹었다고 하자 공이 입을 딱 벌렸다. 그가 통조림을 아랫면이 위로 가도록 뒤집어 내 눈앞에 내밀었다. 그것은 원터치 캔이었다. 통조림 아랫면에 원터치 고리가 부착되어 있었던 것이다. 나도 입을 딱 벌렸다. 세상에 그렇게 쉬운 일을, 통조림을 뒤집어보기만 해도 되었을 것을.

benches in a park near the Chonggye Creek. Kong looks into his cell phone and says people are beginning to throng the Plaza in front of the City Hall. Twitter users are spreading the message every which way that everyone should gather there.

"What're they gonna do there?"

"Well... They probably think it's unfair to just sit and wait for their death."

Kong says if he had known about all of this ahead of time, he would have given up on things like preparing for employment earlier on, and traveled a lot and had slept with women to his heart's content. Then all of a sudden he blurts out:

"Do you know who's the bitterest person in the world at this moment?"

"Well... rich people?"

"The person whose last orthodontics appointment is tomorrow."

I laugh loudly. He continues: the man getting discharged from the army service tomorrow; the college prep student receiving his admission letter tomorrow; the head of a family who's finally able to own a house for the first time tomorrow; the woman giving birth tomorrow; the baby born tomorrow... The people who feel bitter the most

우리는 마주보고 웃었다.

공이 집게손가락을 천천히 고리 안으로 넣었다.

『2013 제4회 젊은작가상 수상작품집』, 문학동네, 2013

aren't those who already have a lot, but those who have a future to await.

"You know, Halley's Comet."

"Yeah, what about it?"

Kong gazes up at the distant sky.

"Will it still come here even after the earth's disappeared?"

He says Halley's Comet passes by the earth every 76 years; and since the last sighting was in 1986, it'll come again in 2062 if calculations are correct. He mutters it's not really fair that he won't be on the earth when the comet comes this time. Since his childhood, he's always imagined himself as an old man in his eighties enjoying a first-hand sighting in 2062.

I just look into my cell phone silently. I can't imagine the world with all of us gone. I can't even believe or imagine the moment of our deaths. It's already four in the afternoon. I get curious all of a sudden. Does Kong remember? The assignment we were given long ago in one of the liberal arts classes—to write about the end of the world? Does he remember my piece that I read to the class? Did he take the hint at the time?

"How long do we have left?"

"Oh—about 14 hours."

I put my cell phone back in my purse. I take out the can of peaches. I tell Kong that I wanted to eat it, but I couldn't because I didn't have a can opener. Then, his jaw drops. He takes the can, turns it upside down, and shows me the underside. It's a one-touch can! The one-touch ring is on the bottom. My jaw drops, too. My God, it could have been so easy! If only I'd turned the can over just once. We look at each other and laugh.

Kong feels for the one-touch ring, and loops his finger through.

Translated by Jeon Miseli

해설

Afterword

종말의 시간 속에 새겨진 어떤 기다림

송종원 (문학평론가)

김미월은 지금까지 지속적으로 시의성 있는 작품들을 발표해왔다. 그녀의 소설은 한국사회의 징후를 포착하기에 늘 좋은 텍스트였으며, 또 한편으로는 대중들이 흥미를 가지고 따라 읽기 쉬운 언어와 생활밀착형 소재들을 꾸준히 발견해왔다. 다시 말해 김미월의 작품을 읽는 일은 지금 한국사회에서 어떤 문제적 징후가 발생하고 있는가를 탐색하는 행위와 다르지 않으며, 또한 저 문제적 징후가 어떤 기미로 생활 속에서 포착되는지를 살필 수 있는 계기를 제공한다.

「아직 일어나지 않은 일」은 여러모로 재미있는 단편소설이다. 우선적으로 독자의 관심을 끄는 것은 작품의

A Possible Wait in Apocalyptic Times

Song Jong-won (literary critic)

Ever since her debut, Kim Mi-wol has steadily produced works relevant to contemporary social circumstances. Each of her stories provides an excellent diagnosis of Korean society. Furthermore, she has constantly strived to discover new material and language accessible for the general public to absolutely fall into. In other words, reading Kim Mi-wol's work amounts to detecting the problematic symptoms in present-day Korean society and offers opportunities to examine how those symptoms manifest themselves in our everyday lives.

"What Has Yet to Happen" is an intriguing short story for a number of reasons. The story's primary source of intrigue, though, is its unique time and

시간적 배경이다. 소설은 작품의 주인공인 '나'가 지난밤에 이상한 꿈을 꾸었다고 믿는 데서 시작한다. 하지만 얼마 지나지 않아 꿈이라고 믿었던 일이 사실임이 밝혀진다. '나'는 만취했던 지난밤에 실제로 지구의 종말 소식을 접했던 것이다. TV와 인터넷 등등의 매체에는 온통 지구 종말에 관한 소식들이 펼쳐지고 있었으며 창밖의 분위기 또한 심상치가 않다. 종말을 몇 시간 앞둔 상황이란 작가에게는 물론 독자들에게까지 흥미로운 상상의 기폭제로 작용한다. 한때 한국 소설에 묵시록적인 풍경이 유행이었던 적은 있었으나 이 소설처럼 지구 종말 몇 시간 전을 직접적인 배경으로 삼은 작품은 없었다.

종말을 앞둔 시간에 벌어지는 여러 주변 인물들의 행태와 주인공이 겪게 되는 사태들의 모습 또한 이 소설의 재미를 배가한다. 가령, 종말을 앞둔 상태에서도 평상심을 잃지 않고 평소대로 소일거리들을 묵묵히 처리하고 자식을 만나러 서울을 올라올 준비를 하는 부모의 모습은 어딘가 희극적이면서도 사실적인 데가 있다. 내일이 종말이기에 어떻게든 먹고 싶은 통조림을 먹겠다며 평소라면 하지 못했을 일을 하는 주인공의 행동, 그

place. The story begins with the protagonist recalling a strange dream the night before. Soon, however, she realizes that it was not a dream but reality. News of the earth's impending doom turns out to be all too true. Mass media outlets continuously broadcast the doomsday news while the street scene outside the narrator and protagonist's window is the picture of post-apocalyptic shock.

This severely imminent catastrophe setting serves, then, as the catalyst to the story and source of its imaginative appeal. At one point, apocalyptic literature was all in vogue in Korea. "What Has Yet to Happen," however, sets itself apart with the extremity of its apocalyptic time frame; there's not even a full day left by the time the protagonist has a full grasp of her situation.

What the protagonist experiences and the other characters do during the last few hours of their lives doubles the fun. For example, the narrator's parents complete their daily chores as usual before traveling to Seoul to join their children, barely losing their composure at all in the face of humanity's mass extinction. The images of the parents are given a subtly comic touch and yet are undeniably rooted in realism. Meanwhile, the protagonist, de-

리고 내일로 미룰 수 없는 택배 일에 최선을 다하는 택배기사의 모습 또한 희극적이면서 어딘가 비극적인 색채의 느낌을 자아낸다. 종말을 앞두고 하는 일이 고작 그런 거라니 싶은 마음에 소설의 중반부까지는 주인공이 여전히 꿈을 꾸고 있는 것은 아닐까 의심스러워질 정도이다.

소설의 중반부가 넘으면 종말 시에 일어날 만한 일들이 직접 목격된다. 라디오 방송에서 DJ가 울음을 터뜨리는 방송사고, 거리에 차를 버리고 가버리는 행인들, 거기에 지구의 종말이 다가왔는데 무슨 일이라도 해야 하지 않겠냐는 심리에 시청에 몰려드는 사람들이나 아수라장이 된 거리, 그리고 대통령의 특별담화 등은 분명 종말 시에 일어날 만한 비일상적 모습들이다. 이중에서 몇 가지 묘사들은 짚고 넘어갈 필요가 있다. 한국에서 서울 시청광장이란 특별한 상징적 의미를 지닌다. 대중들의 다층적인 욕망이 표현되는 장소로서 기능한다는 말이다. 그곳은 월드컵과 같은 국가대항전 경기를 단체로 관람하기 위해 모여드는 장소이면서 동시에 정부의 정책에 반대하거나 자본의 불합리한 처사에 항의하기 위한 노동자들의 집회 장소로도 자주 사용되는 공

termined to eat a can of peaches before the world comes to an end the next day, does things completely out of character for her. The deliveryman tries his best to perform his driver duties even when he knows there is no tomorrow, yet another character with both a comic and tragic touch. The things these characters do with death looming over them are so trivial that, until mid-story at least, the readers are left wondering if the protagonist is still in her dream.

In the second half of the story, however, the protagonist actually witnesses what would likely to happen if the earth were to die the next day: a broadcast mishap in which a DJ bursts into tears; drivers abandoning their cars on the streets, people swarming city hall striving to just do something before the end of the world; streets in disarray; and a somber president special address to increasingly panicked citizens. Among these, some merit our special attention. The City Hall Plaza in Seoul has a symbolic meaning since it functions as a space where the multi-layered desires of the public are often expressed. Large crowds gather in the Plaza to watch international tournaments like the World Cup, raise objections to government poli-

간이다. 그곳에 사람들이 모여든다는 설정은 지구의 종말이라는 상황이 단지 지구로 돌진하는 한 행성으로 인해 벌어진 우연한 사건이 아니라는 점을 암시하는 듯 보인다.

주인공은 소설의 후반부에 와서 정말 지구 종말의 징후가 없었던가를 의심한다. 의심의 내용이 적극적으로 전개되지는 않지만 아마도 주인공의 저 의심은 작가가 지구의 종말이 이 사회의 정치경제적인 문제와 무관하지 않다는 것을 드러내고 싶었던 욕망의 흔적일 것이다. 이 추정은 대통령의 특별담화에 대한 묘사와도 무관하지 않다. 흥미롭게도 작가는 대통령의 실명을 직접 거론하면서 그의 입에서 사과의 마음을 표현하도록 만든다. 물론 곧이어 지구의 종말이 그의 잘못은 아니다라는 서술이 덧붙기는 하지만 한국사회에서 여러 가지 문제를 일으켜 놓고도 사과 한마디 하지 않은 이명박 대통령에 대한 대중들의 원한을 생각해보면, 대통령의 사과 발언과 관련한 묘사의 상징적 의미는 결코 작지 않다.

소설의 결말은 주인공과 그의 친구 사이의 유머러스한 대화로 채워진다. 그중 기다림과 관련한 대화는 의

cies, protest the unfair treatment of laborers etc. The throngs of people gathered here in this story seem to imply that the end of the world will not just be an accidental disaster brought about by a planet hurtling towards the earth.

Later in the story, the protagonist questions if there have ever been any signs of the earth's destruction. Her inquiries do not develop much further but may very well reflect the author's desire to expose how the earth's obliteration would remain relevant to the politico-economic problems of our society. The same inferences may be drawn from the president's special address. Interestingly, the author names the president and then has him later apologize to the citizens. The narrator immediately adds that the end of the earth is not the president's fault. Nevertheless, considering the popular resentment against the former oft-criticized, yet openly unapologetic President Lee Myong-bak, the symbolic significance of Kim's presidential apology can be considered anything but trivial.

The story ends with seemingly humorous chit-chat between the protagonist and her friend. Their dialog begins with the question: Who do you think is the bitterest person in the world right now, given

미심장하다. 지구 종말과 관련해 가장 억울해할 사람은 누구일까라는 질문에 농담 따먹는 식의 대화가 주인공과 친구 사이에 오가다, 결론에 와서는 기다릴 미래가 있는 사람이 제일 억울하겠다는 답에 이른다. 이 질문과 답은 마치 작가가 독자에게 당신은 어떤 미래를 기획해왔고 기다려왔는지를 묻는 듯하다. 한발 더 나아가 해석하자면, 기다릴 미래 내지 소망하는 미래가 없는 이들에게 지구의 종말도 그리 특별한 사건은 아닐 것이라는 전언처럼 들리기도 한다. 미래가 없는 사람의 삶은 이미 종말한 삶을 이어나가는 관습만으로 채워진 것은 아닐까. 아마도 김미월은 이 질문을 붙잡고 지구의 종말을 상상한 작품을 썼을지도 모른다.

the fact that the earth will end the next day? At first, their answers are all half in jest. In the end, however, they reach the conclusion that those who have a future to look forward to must feel the greatest bitterness. The question and their conclusions seem to have been put there by the author to pose another question: what sort of future have you readers planned and what are you waiting for? Here, one wonders if the author is implying that for those who have no future to really wait or aspire after, the end of the world might not be so extraordinary an event, their lives are as good as finished and only by force of habit do they continue to live. Kim Mi-wol may have written about this imaginary end of the world while grappling with this question herself.

비평의 목소리

Critical Acclaim

김미월의 소설은 이야기를 통해 시대현실과 개인의 삶을 동시에 성찰하는 소설문학 특유의 미덕을 유감없이 보여준다. 그의 소설이 범상한 듯 비범하게 느껴지는 것은 화려한 기법과 수사, 파격적인 언어 및 형식 실험을 오히려 절제하면서 이 시대 젊은이들의 삶과 꿈의 맥을 차분히 짚어가는 소설적 작업에 정진하고 있기 때문이다.

한기욱

김미월의 소설이 일깨우는 청년 세대의 소통 불안과 공동체의 상상력 역시 특정 소속의 집단적 정체성이 아

Kim Mi-wol's works fully demonstrate a virtue typical of major literature: the ability to peer into the life of an individual while simultaneously examining the social reality of their time. The reason why Kim's stories feel at once ordinary and extraordinary is that she can serenely ponder the lives and dreams of the young in the contemporary society, while refraining from employing colorful skills, flashy rhetoric, unconventional language, or structural experimentation.

Han Gi-uk

Kim Mi-wol's works deserve our full attention in

닌 익명적이고 자유로운 방식의 관계맺음의 염원을 담아낸다는 점에서 중요한 지형을 그리고 있다. 백수와 루저라는 말로 명명되는 청년세대의 고통과 불안은 그의 소설에서 개인들을 연결하는 작고 따뜻한 위무의 공동체에 대한 환상으로 이어진다. 마니아적인 감수성과 아웃사이드적 특징을 공유했던 '취향의 공동체'로부터 익명의 관계들이 연결하는 '소통의 공동체'를 열망하는 것으로 변모하는 양상은 김미월의 소설에서 잘 드러난다고 할 수 있다.

백지연

김미월은 한 세대에 머물러 있으면서도 세대를 아우를 수 있는 비전을 제시한다. 사실 이것이야말로 문학의 본령이 아닌가? 과거에 누군가 남긴 말과 글이, 그 혹은 그녀가 알지도 못하는 현재의 나로 하여금 진리를 깨닫게 하고 나를 회복시켜주는 것. 감당할 수 없을 것 같았던 고통도 먼 훗날 언젠가 우리를 웃게 할 수 있으리라는 것. 문학이 할 수 있는 일은 뒷사람이 공감하고 위로받을 수 있는 말의 모델을 만드는 일일 것이다. 미래를 향해 열려 있는 김미월의 소설에서, 나는 시들었

that her stories vividly depict the anxiety towards authentic communication so often felt by the younger generation. More importantly, Kim points to an ideal community free from any collective identities. In Kim's stories the pain and anxiety of the present-day youth, occasionally labeled the jobless or low-achieving generation, leads them to a vision of a smaller, more warm-hearted community able to link one individual to another. Marked in Kim's narratives is the aspiration of the youth to transition from the maniacal and exclusionary community of common inclination and sensibilities to a community of free communication among anonymous individuals.

Baek Ji-yeon

Kim Mi-wol presents a vision that can encompass all the generations even while depicting only one of them, which I believe constitutes the true essence of literature. The words left by someone in the past help me, although he or she has never known me, to recuperate and see the truth by giving me the hope that someday I will be able to smile at the unbearable pain of the moment. What literature should do is make verbal archetypes that

다고 생각하고 실망한 문학이 연둣빛 새싹을 수줍고 겸손하게 틔우기 시작한 것을 보고 기뻐한다. 우리의 겨울이 길었기에 우리에게 와준 봄이 더욱 소중하고 고맙다.

허윤진

이제, 2000년대 후반 이후의 젊은 소설은 어떤 움직임을 보여줄 수 있을까? 김미월의 사례는 현대소설이 어떻게 '현대적인 것들'을 매개로 '현대'를 관통해서 나아가는가를 매력적으로 드러낸다. 그는 현대소설의 낯익은 모티프와 주제들을 담담하고 역설적인 방식으로 재구축한다. 가족과 개인의 기억에 대한 익숙한 질문법들을 무대 위에 다시 올려놓고 짐짓 천진스러운 화법으로 그 질문들의 기반을 무너뜨린다. 그것들을 무대에서 끌어내리는 방식이 아니라 그 무대 자체의 균열을 드러내는 방식으로, 김미월은 '가족 이야기'를 허물고 아버지의 유토피아를 외로운 개인들의 최소낙원으로 대체한다.

이광호

can resonate and comfort the hearts of the generations to come. I am happy to see in Kim Mi-wol's writing fiction that remains open towards the future, a green bud in the world of literature that I once considered withered and dead. Our winter has been far too long and so the arrival of spring is that much more appreciated.

Huh Yun-jin

Now, what course will the fiction of the young generation take in the latter half of the 2000s? The case of Kim Mi-wol reveals how the present-day fiction breaks through the modern era, while taking advantage of the modern world. She reconstructs the familiar motifs and themes of modern fiction in a composed and paradoxical fashion. She puts the familiar questions about the memories of the family and the individual back on stage only to destroy the foundation of these questions using her seemingly innocuous style of speech. Her aim is not to drag the familiar questions down from the stage, but to expose the cracks in their foundation, or even, the stage itself. She dismantles the utopia headed by the Father in familial stories to replace it with miniature utopias of lonely individuals.

Lee Kwang-ho

김미월

1977년 강릉에서 태어났다. 고려대학교 언어학과와 서울예술대학교 문예창작학과를 졸업했다. 2004년 세계일보 신춘문예에 「정원에 길을 묻다」가 당선되어 작품 활동을 시작했다. 당시 심사위원의 평은 이러했다. "'정원에 길을 묻다'는 재기가 두드러지는 작품이다. 인터넷상의 해결사 사이트를 운영하는 것으로 현실적 생활을 해결하는 주인공의 일상을 생생히 보여준다. 온라인과 오프라인의 경계가 모호한 삶을 살면서 시멘트 옥상에 공중정원을 가꾸는 것으로 존재 증명을 삼는다는 설정으로 지금, 이 시간을 살아가는 사람들의 내면 정경을 펼쳐 보이는 것은 자못 흥미롭고 시사하는 바가 크다."

등단 이후 그의 작품 활동은 평단의 지속적인 관심을 받았다. 2007년에 출간된 그녀의 첫 단편집 「서울 동굴 가이드」는 경제적 능력과 관련한 불안과 사회적 고립감에 유독 많이 노출되어 있는 한국의 20대 청춘들의 삶을 그리고 있는데, 이 소설집은 한국에서 명망 있는 문

Kim Mi-wol

Kim Mi-wol was born in Gangneung in 1977. After graduating first from Korea University as a linguistics major and then from Seoul Institute of the Arts with a major in creative writing, Kim made her debut with the short story "Asking the Garden for Direction," which won *the Segye Times* sponsored Spring Literary Contest in 2004. At the same time, the judging committee commented: "'Asking the Garden for Direction' demonstrates well the writer's genius. It vividly depicts the everyday life of a protagonist who makes a living by running a trouble-solving broker site on the Internet. As the line between the online and offline blurs, the protagonist tries to prove her existence by keeping a garden on the cement rooftop. The setup is very intriguing and suggestive of the psychological landscape of the people living through the here and now."

Since her debut, Kim Mi-wol has received the unswerving attention of the critics. In 2007, her first collection of short stories *Seoul Cave Guide* was published to much critical acclaim. Many of the

학상 중 하나인 동인문학상의 후보에 오르기도 하였다. 2010년에 출간된 첫 장편소설집 『여덟 번째 방』 역시 작품성을 크게 인정받았다. 경제적인 독립과 본인의 꿈을 위해 지하 단칸방과 옥탑방을 전전하는 한 청춘의 녹록치 않는 삶을 그리고 있는 이 작품으로 김미월은 2011년 신동엽문학상을 받았다. 신동엽문학상 심사위원들은 "현실에 대한 진지한 문학적 응전의 정신과 성과를 높이 평가"한다고 밝힌 바 있다. 2011년에는 두 번째 단편소설집 『아무도 펼쳐보지 않는 책』을 출간하였다. 이 책 역시 김미월 특유의 핍진성 있는 서사와 따뜻한 감성으로 독자와 평단의 좋은 평가를 받았다.

stories in the collection depict the lives of young Koreans in their twenties suffering from a heightened sense of anxiety and social alienation stemming from economic incompetence. This collection was nominated for the Dongin Literary Award, one of the most prestigious literary awards in Korea.

Kim's first full-length novel *The Eighth Room* (2010) also received much recognition for its high literary quality. The novel narrates the formidable life of the young protagonist forced to constantly move from one underground single-room to another, from one rooftop room to another in order to realize his dream while maintaining his economic independence. *The Eighth Room* won the Shin Dong-yeop Literary Award, a highly respected award in the Korean Literary Circles in 2011. The judging committee of the Shin Dong-yeop Literary Award said of her works, "Kim's sincere writer's spirit that constantly seeks to challenge reality is greatly appreciated." Finally, in 2011, her second collection of short stories *Unopened Book* was released to great acclaim from both the readership and the critical world. As in all Kim Mi-wol's works, it was lauded for its heartwarming sensibilities and striking verisimilitude to the world as we see it today.

번역 **전미세리** Translated by Jeon Miseli

한국외국어대학교 동시통역대학원을 졸업한 후, 캐나다 브리티시컬럼비아 대학교 도서관학, 아시아학과 문학 석사, 동 대학 비교문학과 박사 학위를 취득하고 강사 및 아시아 도서관 사서로 근무했다. 한국국제교류재단 장학금을 지원받았고, 캐나다 연방정부 사회인문과학연구회의 연구비를 지원받았다. 오정희의 단편 「직녀」를 번역했으며 그 밖에 서평, 논문 등을 출판했다.

Jeon Miseli is graduate from the Graduate School of Simultaneous Interpretation, Hankuk University of Foreign Studies and received her M.L.S. (School of Library and Archival Science), M.A. (Dept. of Asian Studies) and Ph.D. (Programme of Comparative Literature) at the University of British Columbia, Canada. She taught as an instructor in the Dept. of Asian Studies and worked as a reference librarian at the Asian Library, UBC. She was awarded the Korea Foundation Scholarship for Graduate Students in 2000. Her publications include the translation "Weaver Woman"(***Acta Koreana***, Vol. 6, No. 2, July 2003) from the original short story "Chingnyeo"(1970) written by Oh Jung-hee.

감수 **전승희, 데이비드 윌리엄 홍**

Edited by Jeon Seung-hee and David William Hong

전승희는 서울대학교와 하버드대학교에서 영문학과 비교문학으로 박사 학위를 받았으며, 현재 하버드대학교 한국학 연구소의 연구원으로 재직하며 아시아 문예 계간지 《ASIA》 편집위원으로 활동 중이다. 현대 한국문학 및 세계문학을 다룬 논문을 다수 발표했으며, 바흐친의 『장편소설과 민중언어』, 제인 오스틴의 『오만과 편견』 등을 공역했다. 1988년 한국여성연구소의 창립과 《여성과 사회》의 창간에 참여했고, 2002년부터 보스턴 지역 피학대 여성을 위한 단체인 '트랜지션하우스' 운영에 참여해 왔다. 2006년 하버드대학교 한국학 연구소에서 '한국 현대사와 기억'을 주제로 한 워크숍을 주관했다.

Jeon Seung-hee is a member of the Editorial Board of ***ASIA***, and a Fellow at the Korea Institute, Harvard University. She received a Ph.D. in English Literature from Seoul National University and a Ph.D. in Comparative Literature from Harvard University. She has presented and published numerous papers on modern Korean and world literature. She is also a co-translator of Mikhail Bakhtin's ***Novel and the People's Culture*** and Jane Austen's ***Pride and Prejudice***. She is a founding member of the Korean Women's Studies Institute and of the biannual Women's Studies' journal ***Women and Society*** (1988), and she has been working at 'Transition House,' the first and oldest shelter for battered women in New England. She organized a workshop entitled "The Politics of Memory in Modern Korea" at the Korea Institute, Harvard University, in 2006. She also served as an advising committee member for the Asia-Africa Literature Festival in 2007 and for the POSCO Asian Literature Forum in 2008.

데이비드 윌리엄 홍은 미국 일리노이주 시카고에서 태어났다. 일리노이대학교에서 영문학을, 뉴욕대학교에서 영어교육을 공부했다. 지난 2년간 서울에 거주하면서 처음으로 한국인과 아시아계 미국인 문학에 깊이 몰두할 기회를 가졌다. 현재 뉴욕에서 거주하며 강의와 저술 활동을 한다.

David William Hong was born in 1986 in Chicago, Illinois. He studied English Literature at the University of Illinois and English Education at New York University. For the past two years, he lived in Seoul, South Korea, where he was able to immerse himself in Korean and Asian-American literature for the first time. Currently, he lives in New York City, teaching and writing.

바이링궐 에디션 한국 대표 소설 075
아직 일어나지 않은 일

2014년 6월 6일 초판 1쇄 인쇄 | 2014년 6월 13일 초판 1쇄 발행

지은이 김미월 | **옮긴이** 전미세리 | **펴낸이** 김재범
감수 전승희, 데이비드 윌리엄 홍 | **기획** 정은경, 전성태, 이경재
편집 정수인, 이은혜 | **관리** 박신영 | **디자인** 이춘희
펴낸곳 (주)아시아 | **출판등록** 2006년 1월 27일 제406-2006-000004호
주소 서울특별시 동작구 서달로 161-1(흑석동 100-16)
전화 02.821.5055 | **팩스** 02.821.5057 | **홈페이지** www.bookasia.org
ISBN 979-11-5662-018-1 (set) | 979-11-5662-037-2 (04810)
값은 뒤표지에 있습니다.

Bi-lingual Edition Modern Korean Literature 075
What Has Yet to Happen

Written by Kim Mi-wol I **Translated by** Jeon Miseli
Published by Asia Publishers I 161-1, Seodal-ro, Dongjak-gu, Seoul, Korea
Homepage Address www.bookasia.org I **Tel**. (822).821.5055 I **Fax**. (822).821.5057
First published in Korea by Asia Publishers 2014
ISBN 979-11-5662-018-1 (set) | 979-11-5662-037-2 (04810)

〈바이링궐 에디션 한국 대표 소설〉 작품 목록(1~60)

아시아는 지난 반세기 동안 한국에서 나온 가장 중요하고 첨예한 문제의식을 가진 작가들의 작품들을 선별하여 총 105권의 시리즈를 기획하였다. 하버드 한국학 연구원 및 세계 각국의 우수한 번역진들이 참여하여 외국인들이 읽어도 어색함이 느껴지지 않는 손색없는 번역으로 인정받았다. 이 시리즈는 세계인들에게 문학 한류의 지속적인 힘과 가능성을 입증하는 전집이 될 것이다.

바이링궐 에디션 한국 대표 소설 set 1

분단 Division

01 병신과 머저리-**이청준** The Wounded-**Yi Cheong-jun**
02 어둠의 혼-**김원일** Soul of Darkness-**Kim Won-il**
03 순이삼촌-**현기영** Sun-i Samch'on-**Hyun Ki-young**
04 엄마의 말뚝 1-**박완서** Mother's Stake I-**Park Wan-suh**
05 유형의 땅-**조정래** The Land of the Banished-**Jo Jung-rae**

산업화 Industrialization

06 무진기행-**김승옥** Record of a Journey to Mujin-**Kim Seung-ok**
07 삼포 가는 길-**황석영** The Road to Sampo-**Hwang Sok-yong**
08 아홉 켤레의 구두로 남은 사내-**윤흥길** The Man Who Was Left as Nine Pairs of Shoes-**Yun Heung-gil**
09 돌아온 우리의 친구-**신상웅** Our Friend's Homecoming-**Shin Sang-ung**
10 원미동 시인-**양귀자** The Poet of Wŏnmi-dong-**Yang Kwi-ja**

여성 Women

11 중국인 거리-**오정희** Chinatown-**Oh Jung-hee**
12 풍금이 있던 자리-**신경숙** The Place Where the Harmonium Was-**Shin Kyung-sook**
13 하나코는 없다-**최윤** The Last of Hanak'o-**Ch'oe Yun**
14 인간에 대한 예의-**공지영** Human Decency-**Gong Ji-young**
15 빈처-**은희경** Poor Man's Wife-**Eun Hee-kyung**

바이링궐 에디션 한국 대표 소설 set 2

자유 Liberty

16 필론의 돼지-**이문열** Pilon's Pig-**Yi Mun-yol**
17 슬로우 불릿-**이대환** Slow Bullet-**Lee Dae-hwan**
18 직선과 독가스-**임철우** Straight Lines and Poison Gas-**Lim Chul-woo**
19 깃발-**홍희담** The Flag-**Hong Hee-dam**
20 새벽 출정-**방현석** Off to Battle at Dawn-**Bang Hyeon-seok**

사랑과 연애 Love and Love Affairs

21 별을 사랑하는 마음으로-**윤후명** With the Love for the Stars-**Yun Hu-myong**
22 목련공원-**이승우** Magnolia Park-**Lee Seung-u**
23 칼에 찔린 자국-**김인숙** Stab-**Kim In-suk**
24 회복하는 인간-**한강** Convalescence-**Han Kang**
25 트렁크-**정이현** In the Trunk-**Jeong Yi-hyun**

남과 북 South and North

26 판문점-**이호철** Panmunjom-**Yi Ho-chol**
27 수난 이대-**하근찬** The Suffering of Two Generations-**Ha Geun-chan**
28 분지-**남정현** Land of Excrement-**Nam Jung-hyun**
29 봄 실상사-**정도상** Spring at Silsangsa Temple-**Jeong Do-sang**
30 은행나무 사랑-**김하기** Gingko Love-**Kim Ha-kee**

바이링궐 에디션 한국 대표 소설 set 3

서울 Seoul

31 눈사람 속의 검은 항아리-**김소진** The Dark Jar within the Snowman-**Kim So-jin**
32 오후, 가로지르다-**하성란** Traversing Afternoon-**Ha Seong-nan**
33 나는 봉천동에 산다-**조경란** I Live in Bongcheon-dong-**Jo Kyung-ran**
34 그렇습니까? 기린입니다-**박민규** Is That So? I'm A Giraffe-**Park Min-gyu**
35 성탄특선-**김애란** Christmas Specials-**Kim Ae-ran**

전통 Tradition

36 무자년의 가을 사흘-**서정인** Three Days of Autumn, 1948-**Su Jung-in**
37 유자소전-**이문구** A Brief Biography of Yuja-**Yi Mun-gu**
38 향기로운 우물 이야기-**박범신** The Fragrant Well-**Park Bum-shin**
39 월행-**송기원** A Journey under the Moonlight-**Song Ki-won**
40 협죽도 그늘 아래-**성석제** In the Shade of the Oleander-**Song Sok-ze**

아방가르드 Avant-garde

41 아겔다마-**박상륭** Akeldama-**Park Sang-ryoong**
42 내 영혼의 우물-**최인석** A Well in My Soul-**Choi In-seok**
43 당신에 대해서-**이인성** On You-**Yi In-seong**
44 회색 時-**배수아** Time In Gray-**Bae Su-ah**
45 브라운 부인-**정영문** Mrs. Brown-**Jung Young-moon**

바이링궐 에디션 한국 대표 소설 set 4

디아스포라 Diaspora

46 속옷-**김남일** Underwear-**Kim Nam-il**
47 상하이에 두고 온 사람들-**공선옥** People I Left in Shanghai-**Gong Sun-ok**
48 모두에게 복된 새해-**김연수** Happy New Year to Everyone-**Kim Yeon-su**
49 코끼리-**김재영** The Elephant-**Kim Jae-young**
50 먼지별-**이경** Dust Star-**Lee Kyung**

가족 Family

51 혜자의 눈꽃-**천승세** Hye-ja's Snow-Flowers-**Chun Seung-sei**
52 아베의 가족-**전상국** Ahbe's Family-**Jeon Sang-guk**
53 문 앞에서-**이동하** Outside the Door-**Lee Dong-ha**
54 그리고, 축제-**이혜경** And Then the Festival-**Lee Hye-kyung**
55 봄밤-**권여선** Spring Night-**Kwon Yeo-sun**

유머 Humor

56 오늘의 운세-**한창훈** Today's Fortune-**Han Chang-hoon**
57 새-**전성태** Bird-**Jeon Sung-tae**
58 밀수록 다시 가까워지는-**이기호** So Far, and Yet So Near-**Lee Ki-ho**
59 유리방패-**김중혁** The Glass Shield-**Kim Jung-hyuk**
60 전당포를 찾아서-**김종광** The Pawnshop Chase-**Kim Chong-kwang**